ARCHETYPES OF HUMAN EXISTENCE

ABOUT THE AUTHOR

JOHN MUCAI HOLDS A PH.D. in Business Administration from the University of Nairobi. He is a Certified Public Accountant of Kenya too. He is an alumnus of United States International University, where he graduated with an MSc in Management and Organizational Development and cum laude in BSc in Information Systems & Technology. He retired from Coca-Cola East & Central Africa Ltd in 2017 and has since been pursuing various hobbies and entrepreneurial interests.

ARCHETYPES OF HUMAN EXISTENCE

A New Perspective

John Mucai

"The only way to deal with an unfree world is to become so absolutely free that your very existence is an act of rebellion."

—ALBERT CAMUS

For any further information, contact John Muigai Mucai at the following address:
P.O. Box 2069 - 00606, Nairobi, Kenya. Email: johnmucai@gmail.com

Cover design by Linda Matama

ISBN: 978-9914-40-015-1

CONTENTS

FOREWORD

"ARCHETYPES OF EXISTENCE" is the tenth book in the MUCAI Quick Read series. This series caters to readers seeking lighthearted and thought-provoking entertainment, perfect for a bus, train, cruise, or plane ride, a relaxing beach day in Mombasa, or simply unwinding at home after a long day.

The series spans a diverse range of topics to stimulate the reader's intellect:

- Humorous biographical tales
- Chronicles of captivating historical events
- Narratives of extraordinary scientific ideas
- Journeys toward spiritual enlightenment
- Intrigues in business
- Strategy
- Thought-provoking philosophical ideas

The MUCAI Quick Read series aims to inspire readers to adopt a fresh and positive perspective on life. For more information on the series, please visit *mucaiquickread.com*.

PREFACE

NO TWO OF THE MORE THAN seven billion people inhabiting the earth are exactly the same. Even tweens have differences. Nature has bestowed unique attributes on each of us. And yet, the behavior of human beings can be reduced to a few archetypes.

At the heart of the matter, each human being is one single entity comprised of a mind and a physical body – a mind that yearns for happiness and a body that longs for sustenance. And the interplay of these two needs creates the different archetypes of humans. This book explores a few of the archetypes. It discusses how the ideas around archetypes converge to offer a new perspective on fundamental questions that existentialists have grappled with for ages.

The people described in the second chapter of this book are entirely fictitious. However, the characters are real and live among us. You may recognize some of them in your local community, your network of friends, or even in other human networks to which you are directly or indirectly connected.

ACKNOWLEDGMENTS

The Almighty God has been the shining guiding light throughout my life, even in this book project. I will always remain steadfastly thankful to Him.

This book would not have been possible without the ongoing unshakeable support of my wife, Susan, my son, Allan, and my daughter, Anne. I am deeply grateful to them.

I would also like to thank Teddy Muhia and Nzisa Kattambo for reviewing the book and offering invaluable feedback.

PART I

Introduction

CHAPTER 1

Introduction

*"The proper function of man is to live, not to exist.
I shall not waste my days in trying to prolong
them. I shall use my time."*
—Jack London

Throughout my working career, I have visited and stayed in many places. While each place was distinct in its unique way, I could not help but conclude that all the people I met were essentially the same. They were the same regardless of ethnic background, religion, or education. The subtle distinctions emerged when people started putting various labels on themselves or others.

Some things that happen at kindergarten are interesting indicators of who we are as human beings. Please join me on a time travel trip on the first day of kindergarten.

The only outfit required for the journey is your set of adult observation lenses.

* * *

If you observe keenly, you will notice that every newcomer to kindergarten assumes a certain status depending on the person who dropped them off at the kindergarten, the kind of car the person was driving, or the other mode of transport they used to bring the newcomer to kindergarten.

One kid is brought in a top-of-the-range SUV driven by a young lady. The eyes of all the kids descend on the newcomer. The kid must obviously be from a wealthy family. From the moment the kid steps on the pavement of the kindergarten grounds, he is a hero. He is accorded the kind of respect deserving of young aristocrats like him.

Another kid walks in through the main gate accompanied by an 80-year-old man struggling to support himself on a walking stick. Everyone in the kindergarten, including the teachers, assumes the kid has been brought to kindergarten by his grandfather. It does not matter that the 80-year-old man may be the kid's real father. As far as the other kindergarten kids are concerned, the newcomer is and will remain the son of a "grandfather."

Yet another kid is brought in an old cranky station wagon, with some goats standing between the front and the back seat. The person in the driver's seat is a disheveled middle-aged man.

That combination instantly earns the new kid a nickname befitting his status as a "farmer" – probably a fun nickname, but undoubtedly one with demeaning connotations. And there is nothing that the kid can do about it. She will have to live with the label for the duration of her days at kindergarten. That label will become part of her. It will be written with indelible ink in the DNA of her psyche and influence her worldview in the days ahead.

You and the other kids will graduate from kindergarten and join a primary school in about two years. The world will become even more interesting. All of you will acquire even more labels. Some labels will uplift your character; others will push you back.

For example, if you decide to partake of more than the recommended servings of food, other kids will give you the label "fatso." This label may force you to react in different ways. You could become aggressive to prevent the label from sticking to you. This aggression could manifest itself in the form of pinching the ears of anyone who dares call you "fatso." Pinching another kid's ears will earn you yet another label, bully. And if luck is not on your side, you could get into trouble with teachers. The teachers will memorialize the label in your personal records and even add that you are a troublemaker. And that troublemaker record will follow you for the rest of your life.

A New Perspective

Thank God that the FBI and similar agencies do not check early primary school records before issuing certificates of good conduct; otherwise, the simple action of pinching another kid's ears for calling you fatso because you had over-indulged in sweet things over a two-month period would potentially result in your missing a great job opportunity.

* * *

Perhaps in the next 100 years, a machine will scan the DNA of an individual's psyche and unravel the number and nature of labels that one has accumulated over time.

We are all the same, constantly wiggling in different directions and doing different things, or being pushed around by others to clean up our existing labels or trying to acquire new, more appealing ones.

The label clean-up and acquisition processes are endless. They end when a few labels are read out in one's eulogy when departing from this world of labels.

* * *

If you spare a moment to consider the people you know, you will not fail to see that at the core of their being are the different labels they have acquired over time by virtue of their place of birth, the status of their parents, the schools they have attended, the people they have interacted with, the books they have read, and the influences they have absorbed from others. Given the heterogeneous nature of human beings, it is not difficult to see that we can group people into a few different archetypes based on their labels.

In the next chapter, we will explore the lives of several fictitious characters to glimpse the shaping of their psyches' DNA. This exploration will give us a foundation for formulating our ideas of archetypes in the subsequent chapter.

But one may ask, what is the point of it all? Why even bother classifying people into archetypes? These questions are important and invite even more fundamental questions that existentialist philosophers have grappled with over millennia: What is the meaning of life? Who am I? What is the meaning of existence?

In Part III of the book, we will examine the perspectives of several renowned existentialist philosophers.

We will marry our archetypes with existentialist philosophical ideas to derive a new perspective in Part IV. Hopefully, a perspective that will bring us closer to the ultimate truth many people have sought for decades and centuries.

PART II

Archetypes

CHAPTER 2

Archetypes of Human Existence

"By learning to recognize when your own archetypes are taking over, it's easier to observe when other people are living from their shadow selves."
—*Catherine Carrigan*

THE OXFORD ENGLISH DICTIONARY DEFINES archetype as "a very typical example of a certain person or thing." This definition is the one we use in this book. It refers to a type of person based on certain personality characteristics. The archetypes presented in this book are a sample to provide context for the subsequent discussion of existentialism and the author's answers to a few fundamental questions existentialists have been grappling with for decades.

* * *

Observer

THE RAY OF LIGHT COMING through the furthest end of the window pierced the footboard of the maternity bed like a sharp, translucent blade. The brightness of the morning sunlight added to the magic of the moment.

The baby was sleeping in a comfortable cot wrapped in immaculate white clothes. She looked like an angel. Tabitha leaned over from her maternity bed and peered into the cot. She momentarily blushed as she took in the most miraculous experience of her life.

It was June 25, 1963, in the Godfrey Ashcomb Maternity Hospital in Hampstead, London. In keeping with Tabitha Oluoch's Luo family tradition, the parents named the child Akinyi because the child was born in the morning. This first label was automatic. A function of tradition carried forward for several generations by Tabitha's community.

It was as if the name had crystallized from the ether as Akinyi emerged from her mother's womb. And yet, Akinyi would only learn about it several months later. Even so, she would assimilate the knowledge only gradually, unlike the automatic embossment of the tradition on the DNA of her psyche at the instance of her maternal entry into the world. How odd!

Akinyi could not relinquish the name. Family traditions had decided for her centuries before June 25, 1963.

Akinyi's mother was from the Luo tribe in Kenya, while her father, James Mackintosh, was a Scotsman from Dundee. James could not understand the naming of the child based on a tradition that he could not relate to directly. He would have preferred Priscilla, Ebony, or Meredith. But he had been overtaken by an African tradition.

Tabitha and James were doting parents, ensuring Akinyi received the best upbringing possible. The utmost loving and tender care started on day one of Akinyi's arrival home from the maternity hospital. Her cot was well decorated with fancy child toys. Several teddy bears were in the room, many of them from friends of the Mackintoshs'. Many of the items would only become of value to Akinyi in 1965.

It was all happiness and joy around beautiful little Akinyi. Even Jasper, the family dog, participated in the fanfare, albeit a little jealous due to the attention that Akinyi received from Tabitha and James.

Although not particularly religious, James and Tabitha were keen to ensure that Akinyi followed the correct, righteous path through her childhood. They attended church school for six weeks to re-establish their church membership in readiness for Akinyi's baptism. It was a splendid journey that reintroduced James and Tabitha to their religious faiths that had worn off over time through neglect.

Akinyi was baptized Priscilla six months after her birth, on Christmas Day 1963. It was a memorable occasion witnessed by several relatives of her parents from Kenya and Scotland. According to church tradition, the pastor solemnized the baptism by dipping Akinyi's head in a small water-filled basin. The pastor removed her head from the water, held her head in his right palm, and with Akinyi screaming at the top of her voice, said:

"Priscilla Akinyi Mackintosh, I baptize you in the name of the Father, the Son, and the Holy Spirit. Amen. Jesus has received you into his flock, and I mark you with the sign of his cross."

The minister then made a sign of the cross on the face of Priscilla Akinyi Mackintosh.

The ceremony lasted thirty minutes, during which Tabitha and James made several vows, committing to shepherd Akinyi the Christian way.

The baptism was a flowless happenstance to which the congregation cheered loudly. Without her knowledge, Akinyi had entered a fraternity whose membership extended beyond her infantile imagination, something that she would only realize a few years later. By going through the baptism, Akinyi acquired a new identity that would distinguish her from people of other faiths. Once again, it was something that she could not freely abandon.

Her parents and the community around her had considered it essential, as a rite of passage, for her membership of the Christian congregation in Hampstead.

The new label was to remain permanently emblazoned on the amorphous DNA of her psyche - a label predestined to be attached to her based on a tradition that started in the Middle East several centuries ago, albeit a label with a humongous difference from her first label, Akinyi.

While predetermined in the manner in which it was emblazoned on her, the second label had some inbuilt flexibility. The parents had been free to choose it arbitrarily as long as it was acceptable to the church, preferably a name from the Bible.

Priscilla Akinyi Mackintosh was now a child of mixed descent (Kenyan and Scottish), a member of the Hamstead community, and a Christian.

Over time, she would transition through infancy, toddlerhood, schoolgirlhood, adolescence, young adulthood, adulthood, and old age. A unique evolution of her psychology would mark each stage. She would progressively experience several dichotomies of psychological development: trust vs. mistrust, autonomy vs. shame and doubt, initiative vs. guilt, industry vs. inferiority, identity vs. role confusion, intimacy vs. isolation, generativity vs. stagnation, and integrity vs. despair.[1] Throughout this period, she would acquire multiple other labels.

* * *

Priscilla Akinyi's eighth birthday was a significant turning point in her life. Her mother had organized a big birthday party. The list of guests read like an attempt to re-create the family trees of the Oluochs and the Mackintoshes. However, only a few UK-based members of the Oluoch family could attend the party because of travel challenges. They were outnumbered almost five to one by the Mackintoshes.

During the merry-making in the late afternoon, one of the guests from Scotland, Sarah Ainsley, who was seated on a sofa near the coffee table on which Tabitha had placed the birthday cake, made a snide remark about Priscilla's skin complexion. She said:

"You look beautiful, sweety. What chocolate face cream did you apply this morning?"

Sarah was a little tipsy. She had made the remark in jest, but it emerged from her intoxicated mouth like a thoughtless insult.

Priscilla was still a kid, but she recognized the venom in the remark. She quickly dipped her hand into the half-eaten birthday chocolate cake and smeared it on Sarah's face. Priscilla then turned away and rushed towards her room.

The tipsy Scotswoman shouted in anger: "What a brat! How can she do that to me?"

Tabitha was several feet away and was interrupted by the commotion.

"What has happened?" Tabitha asked loudly.

"Your little monkey has smeared chocolate on my face. What a brat. You need to punish her thoroughly." The now ugly-looking, drunken Scotswoman uttered

"Where is Priscilla?" Tabitha screamed, walking hurriedly towards Priscilla's room, temporarily suspending her anger triggered by Sarah's abusive remark about Priscilla.

Priscilla had curled herself like a ball on her little bed. There were brown marks on her face from the chocolate birthday cake. She was sobbing.

"What happened, honey?" Tabitha asked.

"She insulted me, mum! She said! She said! That I had applied chocolate cream on my face."

This was the second time that Tabitha had encountered a situation in which someone had tried to demean her child by reminding the child of her unusual skin color.

Priscilla Akinyi Mackintosh was gradually acquiring another demeaning label, a half-caste. Some insensitive individuals labeled her black to emphasize her difference from other "normal" human beings in London.

Tabitha was livid. She could not accept it anymore. She moved swiftly back into the living room, where the guests congregated near the half-eaten birthday cake and spoke in murmurs.

Tabitha did not exercise any restraint. She pointed her forefinger at tipsy Sarah and ordered her out of the house.

"How dare you denigrate my daughter in that manner, Sarah? Please leave my house immediately. And I never want to see you ever again."

"Tabitha, please calm down, please!" James, who had been outside the house during the momentary commotion, said.

Tabitha had started sobbing and could not control her tears by this time.

She insisted that Sarah leave the premises.

Sarah walked out, murmuring something inaudible due to the loud voices that had now filled the air, voices venting out different sentiments about the altercation that had just occurred.

After Sarah had left, Tabitha's relatives tried their best to comfort her.

For a brief moment, it appeared the two sets of families had re-grouped into two different camps.

The tension in the room was so high that if lit with a matchstick, it could have easily burst into flames.

Meanwhile, Priscilla Akinyi Mackintosh was still alone in her room, sobbing on her little bed. People had given her new demeaning labels that were gradually crystallizing in her psyche's DNA: chocolate face, brat, and a little monkey. Some people mentioned some labels in her absence, but she heard them.

Priscilla was just a little kid, but she now had to bear the weight of a nasty societal attitude - all by herself. Her parents could protect her but could not be at her side every minute of her waking life.

She was not even an adolescent but was more confused than an adult.

None of the kids in her small circle of friends at Hampstead and at school had said anything that upset her about her complexion, but she now wondered whether her friends had just been acting polite.

The seeds of suspicion had been sown in a young mind by a tipsy, senseless Scotswoman.

* * *

During the days that followed, Priscilla Akinyi Mackintosh became increasingly reserved. Her enthusiasm in class and on the playing field significantly declined. No amount of encouragement from her parents and teachers seemed to work. People had punctured a small part of her young soul almost beyond repair.

Priscilla's problem had a serious effect on her parents. They were no longer the happy, bubbly couple they had been ten years earlier. A certain distance had begun to emerge, evident from intermittent quarrels over trivial matters interspersed with periodic mutual snide remarks.

* * *

The seven years in school were a challenging time for Priscilla Akinyi Mackintosh. She resolved to keep a safe distance from those who exhibited even minor signs of unpleasantness. She preferred to keep her head low and move with the flow. This character trait seemed to have been completely ingrained in her psyche. The trait remained part of her being throughout high school.

She did not have many friends. What seemed to give her consolation was periodic walks in the meadows, woodlands, and swimming ponds of Hampstead Heath. Something about the natural environment gave her tremendous solace and bliss.

Her performance in high school was borderline. She managed to score just enough credits to join university. She attended a university in south London to pursue a course in environmental science.

The university environment was vibrant and allowed her the freedom to exercise her mind. But nothing seemed to heal the early childhood wounds. She made a few friends but was careful not to cross the path of anyone who could hurt her feelings. She did not join any student groups or social clubs, preferring to dip her head into books, with most of her time spent in the library.

After four years at university, Priscilla graduated with a first-class honors degree in environmental science. She enrolled in the graduate program and earned a master's degree in environmental management.

A few months after graduation, Priscilla secured a job with an international non-governmental organization that was carrying out several environment conservation projects in different parts of the world.

In June 1991, Priscilla married her work colleague, Amos Prudence. She currently lives in London and is a doting mother to a boy and two beautiful girls.

* * *

In her private moments, Priscilla Akinyi Mackintosh often spends hours pondering on the emptiness that has marked her life since childhood. She feels trapped by circumstances. Although the angst caused by unsolicited remarks about her skin complexion has subsided, she still feels like an outsider.

She is neither a Kenyan nor a Scot. She is something in between. Neither community seems to offer her genuine recognition as one of its members, as an equal. There is always something missing in the relationship that is hard to pinpoint.

She has occasionally poured out her discontent to her husband, Amos, but Amos is too quick to judge and describes her as overly sensitive. He loves her dearly and encourages her to stand tall, irrespective of what others say about her. He always reminds her that her children are in the same situation and that it would be insensitive and border on the selfish to brood about her situation continually.

Priscilla prefers to remain a knowing observer of the world around her. She is hesitant to interfere with the flow of things around her.

Loser

THOMAS KAMAU WAS BORN IN Kangema, about 100 kilometers northeast of Nairobi. He was born into a family of humble means but a family full of pride in their cultural Kikuyu heritage.

Kamau's father, Njoroge Kimani, was a respected local community member, primarily because of his deep knowledge of Kikuyu culture. He was a staunch Kikuyu elder who doubled as an elder in the local church. However, his close friends felt that his leadership positions in the Kikuyu Council of Elders and the church had encroached a little too far in his role as a father. He was famous in the local village as a disciplinarian.

There was a story that did the rounds, albeit slightly exaggerated, that whenever he entered his house after his daily chores, all his children would scamper to their bedrooms. People said he had one unique rule in his home: that children would only be seen and not heard. This sentiment may have been an exaggeration, but it partly explained why Thomas Kamau was so close to his mother and not his father.

As Kamau was growing up in the Njoroge household, traditions compelled him to go through all the prescribed life stages. Firstly, he had to endure life as a boy in the village - this meant that he was subject to disciplinary action by any parent within the village, whether the parent was his father or mother.

Kamau frequently narrated to his friends an event when he and two other 10-year-old boys had decided to go to the local town center, about three kilometers from their village. About halfway on their journey, they met a gentleman named King'ori wa Macharia. King'ori interrogated them intently, seeking to find out the destination of their journey and its purpose. Kamau and his friends lied that Njoroge had sent them to buy paraffin. Unfortunately for the boys, there were two gaping holes in their story: firstly, they did not have even a single cent to buy the paraffin; secondly, they did not have a jar to carry it.

The lies had resulted in instant justice from Kingo'ri. He used a makeshift cane obtained from the vines of a tree in a nearby bush. After just three lashes, the kids spilled the beans that they were lying. At that point, Kingori said he would double the number of lashes. The first set of lashes he had administered was to cover the primary infraction of attempting to go to Kangema town center without their parent's permission. The second set of lashes was to teach Kamau and his friends the seriousness of lying to an elder.

After the lashes, Kamau and his friends-in-crime trooped back to the village, crying at the top of their voices and holding their backsides to reduce the pain sustained from the severe lashes.

That was not all. King'ori subsequently reported the children to their respective parents. For some of them, that was when the real punishment started. Kamau was pinched on the cheeks, knocked on the head several times with bare knuckles, and forced to go to bed that night without eating dinner.

Such incidents instilled discipline in children in the village and sustained an atmosphere of tremendous respect for the village elders.

* * *

When Kamau reached the age of ten, people in the village started referring to him, in an almost derogatory way, *kĩhĩĩ*. The *kĩhĩĩ* label was for any young boy who had not undergone the traditional Kikuyu circumcision ritual. Boys were never old enough to admit it, but the title *kihii* was a stigma they dreamed of relinquishing sooner rather than later.

The life of a *kĩhĩĩ* was quite rough. The community assigned *kĩhĩĩs* different menial tasks, including herding livestock. For this reason, almost every *kihii* looked forward to the day they would undergo the rites of passage to become a *mwanake*, a circumcised young man.

A *mwanake* was the warrior class of the tribe. The community respected him. Further, the community expected him to be a brave man whose primary role was to protect the tribe in the event of an attack by enemies.

Kamau became a *mwanake* in 1965, just before joining high school, in a boarding school located ten kilometers from Kangema town.

This transition made him feel very proud of himself. He was full of confidence, manifested in his vigorous participation in class and the sports field.

But there was a problem. His background was heavily steeped in tradition. There were limits to what he could and could not do, even as a *mwanake*. He was expected to be of utmost good behavior and always show great respect to his elders, irrespective of their social status. This character trait made Kamau much liked by his teachers in high school for his excellent behavior and the respect he displayed to the teachers.

But perhaps his disciplinarian father had taken things a little too far because, despite his good behavior, Kamau had seething anger deep down in his heart. It was a time bomb waiting to explode. As he grew into a strong young man, he started looking for opportunities to rebel, a way to vent anger that had accumulated in his system for many years.

During his third year in high school, he started hob-knobbing with students one class ahead of him – the ones who were popular for their macho attitude. They were all smokers. And it was not long before Kamau himself became a smoker. Initially, smoking made him feel like the elders who smoked in the village.

On one unfortunate occasion, a teacher caught one of his friends with cigarettes. The school principal subjected the boy to severe punishment. The boy buckled under interrogation and revealed all his smoking friends. The principal suspended the boy, Kamau, and other smokers from school.

Kamau did not go home after suspension. He could not risk the absolute wrath of his father, Njoroge. He spent the two weeks of suspension living as a vagabond in the streets of Kangema, occasionally sneaking into the homes of his friends for a meal.

When he returned to school, he was disheveled and emaciated. The teachers did not discover that he had never gone home. They assumed that he had suffered the lesson for his misdeeds from his father, famous in the neighborhood for his ruthlessness.

But the suspension had dealt an indelible mark on Kamau's performance and enthusiasm. He spent endless hours copying notes from his friends.

His performance in the final year of high school was a struggle, too. When the final exams came, his performance was mediocre. He did not get good enough grades to join a university.

He later enrolled in a village Polytechnic where he studied masonry. After graduation, he moved to Nairobi to live with his uncle, a building contractor. There was never a shortage of masonry jobs, but the pay was horrible. But there was not much that Kamau could do about it. He had to live from hand to mouth as a mason.

* * *

While living with his uncle in Nairobi, Kamau met Dorcas Mweni, a housemaid from the Ukambani region. They married after one year.

Today, Kamau, Dorcas, and their two children live in a one-bedroom flat at Dandora. Kamau earns enough to feed the family, but times are always hard.

Kamau spends endless hours thinking about his days in high school and the mistakes he committed by succumbing to the influence of troublemakers. When he attends social gatherings back home, he is always apprehensive for fear of meeting one of his former schoolmates who went to university and got a decent-paying job after graduation.

During political campaigns that occur every five years in the country, Kamau abandons masonry for a few weeks to join politicians who were his former schoolmates. Kamau is always confident of making a few thousand shillings as tips from the politicians.

His lack of university education is a significant drain on his self-esteem.

* * *

In moments of self-reflection, Kamau always seems to gravitate back to the days of his life as a young boy when he suffered hardship because he was a *kĩhĩĩ*. He bitterly recalls the harsh punishment he received from his father, which seemed to have dented his self-confidence as a boy. He reflects on the strict traditional norms he was supposed to follow as he transitioned from a *kĩhĩĩ* to a *mwanake*. He sees traditions as handcuffs that prevent him from acting freely and to his full potential.

And worst of all, he deeply regrets following a group of smokers who vicariously destroyed his chances of doing well in school. He feels a gap in his life. He is unable to shake off feelings of being a loser.

Zombie

IT IS SAID THAT WHEN SALIM CHOKWE WAS born, all the five nurses on duty in the maternity ward on that memorable day had to stop what they were doing to assist in his delivery. This was said partly in jest because you could never get Salim to do anything without pushing him. And he would push back as best as he could, never seeing life's positive side.

Salim Chokwe was born in August 1970 in Malindi. His father was a wealthy businessman with a large wholesale shop in Malindi and a grain-milling plant at Mambrui. His father was a traditional Swahili man who had married four wives and had fifteen children. Salim was the only son of his father's youngest and favorite wife.

By all accounts, Salim was a spoilt child. The closest description of his character was "brat extraordinaire." During his entire primary school education, Salim was taken to school by his mother, Halima, usually in the latest SUV model. His mother would also arrive several minutes before school closing time and wait for him in the car.

Salim occasionally passed via the mall with his mum during the trip home. While at the mall, he would indulge in delicious snacks such as *mahamri* and *kashata*. Most of the time, he would carry a cone of vanilla ice cream, which he would eat slowly while seated in the back seat of the SUV on the way home with his mum.

His mother loved him dearly. He would refer to him jokingly as *Bwanaangu Salim* (my husband, Salim).

But too much of a good thing can sometimes take its toll. When he was in standard eight, Salim lost three of his molars. And his front teeth changed color. They turned to the color of Swiss chocolate due to the over-consumption of sweets. You could not tell his back from his front when he was standing. He had acquired the shape of a balloon-like cartoon. It was a blessing that he was not required to wear a school tie due to the hot weather in Malindi – otherwise, it would have made him look like a penguin. Strangely enough, these physical attributes did not bother his doting mother, Halima, in the least. On the contrary, she seemed to love and spoil him even more.

On the other hand, the other family members were not so complimentary in their attitude. They nicknamed Salim *kifaru wa Malindi* (the rhinoceros of Malindi.) Halima was well aware of the derogatory language used behind her back. She occasionally lashed back at her co-wives for it, accusing them of jealousy of her and her son.

* * *

Because of his desire to calm things in his house, Mzee Athumani, Salim's father, decided to take Salim to a boarding school for high school education. And that is when Salim suddenly came face-to-face with nasty reality.

He was dropped off at the school at around 3:00 p.m. By 4:00 p.m., he had transformed into a spectacle. Half of the older boys in the school surrounded him and looked at him as if he were an animal in a zoo. They had never seen such a huge human specimen.

The old students teased Salim *katumbo* (pot belly), roller, and several other derogatory names. Salim could not have it. He ran to the headmaster's house to report the students. Salim, being the son of one of the wealthiest men in the region, the headmaster, acted swiftly to address the issue. All the students who had insulted Salim were severely punished.

But obesity had become a big handicap for Salim. He could not participate in major sporting activities. It would have been a little dangerous for his health anyway.

His academic performance was not satisfactory either. He had been used to a personal tutor at home. This service was no longer available at boarding school. And he had grown too lazy to push himself into action.

Salim grew into an almost docile individual. But he did not seem to care. He was the son of a rich man. It was obvious he harbored the belief that no matter the outcome of his schooling, he would go back to his father's business and continue with life, as usual, free of any major earthly problems.

Perhaps because of the spoilt lifestyle since he was a small kid, Salim was "always right about everything." Everything he said was right. This attitude was highly irritating to teachers.

Salim flanked his high school exams, but he did not care less.

After leaving high school, Salim's father hired him as the manager of one of the grain mills in Malindi. He still works there as a manager.

A New Perspective

* * *

It is said that nothing has changed for the better since Salim became the manager of the Msasani Maize Mill. He reports for duty at 9:30 a.m. at the earliest, goes for a lunch break at 11:30 a.m., returns at 3:00 p.m., and closes for the day at 4:00 p.m.

But in recent years, Salim has started worrying about his future. His father is getting old, and Salim already sees the emergence of intense succession competition from his more-educated half-brothers. He is worried because he squandered his chances of pursuing higher education. He regrets his cavalier attitude about education in earlier years. He knows his father would not have hesitated to take him to the best university, but he squandered that chance.

Salim has few genuine friends. He knows he needs to marry soon, but he has not met anyone good enough for him. Deep inside, he knows that his attitude puts many people off. Many times, he feels like a purposeless zombie.

Leader

ALBERT SAHA WAS BORN IN Nakuru, Kenya on January 10, 1959. He was the firstborn in a family of six children. His father, Mzee Kimalel, passed away when Albert was fourteen. His mother suffered a sudden stroke upon learning of the death. She remained in ill health for two more years before passing away, too. Albert pushed himself to the extremes to feed his siblings. The odds were terrible, but he overcame them.

It was strange how everything seemed to have collapsed within only two years. Albert's father was a successful farmer in the Rift Valley of Kenya. He owned a farm that was the envy of all his friends. It was 1,000 acres of fertile agricultural land on which Mzee Kimalel grew wheat and barley, occasionally interchanging with maize and potatoes to capitalize on the prevailing market trends.

However, starting in 1970, the wheat crop failed due to bad weather for three consecutive years. In the fourth year, Kimalel decided to risk it all. He borrowed 50 million shillings to up-scale production on his farm. But he was not lucky. He experienced a fourth straight year of crop failure. He was unable to repay the loan. The bank repossessed his land, leaving him completely bankrupt. He died of heart failure shortly after that.

There was suspicion that mafia-like individuals, working in cahoots with some corrupt bank officials and auctioneers, may have caused his death and that the news about heart failure was just a cover-up.

* * *

Suddenly, the children who were in expensive private schools had to abandon those schools and join public schools. The even more challenging part was finding a daily hot meal. But Albert rose to the occasion and ensured his siblings had something to eat daily.

* * *

Albert had always been very close to his father. He had learned quite at an early age how to secure the best prices for farm produce. He had also learned the importance of providing value-adding services to customers. So, when his father's farming empire collapsed, he discovered that by hiring a *mkokoteni* (wagon), he could visit the main farmer's market in Nakuru town at 4:00 am, buy produce at rock-bottom prices, and deliver the produce to traders in a smaller market at Kaloleni.

Traders at Kaloleni were happy that Albert had saved them an early morning trip to the main farmer's market and paid him well for his service. He built sufficient trust with the traders. They rarely asked questions about the prices he asked for the produce.

It was almost miraculous that Albert still found time to attend school and observe punctuality. It was as if he had developed a new internal body clock that could be adjusted at will.

He worked hard in class and was quick to volunteer to lead an initiative when the situation presented itself. He became the captain of the school's football team and started a debating club, in which he was a very active participant. He developed his oratory skills considerably.

Albert passed his secondary school education with flying colors. He was then admitted to university to study engineering, and he received a full scholarship from one of the country's equipment manufacturers.

He joined the University Students Union, where he worked as treasurer and was appointed Chairman during his third year there.

Albert graduated with a first-class degree in mechanical engineering. The company that had given him a scholarship offered him a full-time job as an assistant production manager. Eight years later, he was in the C-suite as the company's Managing Director.

* * *

Albert was never content with his educational progress until all his siblings had joined public universities. Strangely enough, he did not feel contented even after that accomplishment.

At some point, he felt the world was just an endless rat race. What was the point of it all if, in the end, one would exit from this world without carrying with them even a single cent or a simple piece of clothing? According to him, life was hollow. Enjoying music, playing golf, and other earthly pleasures was only momentary. Even his recognition as the leader of his church choir was not enough. A vacuum was always left after engaging in his favorite activities or assuming a particular role. Despite all that he had done for his family and the other accomplishments of his life, he was still a sad-hearted human being. But he had clearly distinguished himself as a leader.

Activist

THE IMAGE OF THE HOODED lady on the television screen looked strangely familiar. Who was she, and why was she in handcuffs? The questions raced through Alex Murungo's mind. It could not be Dorcas, surely! He had just bid her farewell as she returned to college the previous day.

These thoughts triggered perspiration and sweating in the armpits, a strange phenomenon Alex had never experienced. The phone call from Jane, Dorcas's roommate at college, confirmed Murungo's fears.

* * *

Dorcas was the only child of the Murungo family. She was born in Machakos, 50 kilometers from Nairobi, where Murungo and his wife worked as doctors in the Provincial Hospital.

Dorcas was bubbly from the time she was an infant. Her grandmother, Syombua, grew extremely fond of her. Syombua would travel from upcountry often to meet her namesake, little Dorcas Syombua.

On a few occasions when Dorcas was older and did not require close supervision, her parents would take her upcountry to Masii to be with her grandmother. And it had become evident to the Murungos that the grandmother would not exercise any restraint in spoiling her granddaughter. After all, she hwas the only granddaughter who had inherited her name.

But the Murungos would eventually pay the price for their daughter's close attachment to her grandmother. They were very busy in their professional lives as doctors. Any assistance from the grandmother in raising their only child was a significant advantage, and they greatly appreciated it. But they did not notice the subtle changes in Dorcas's life.

As Dorcas transitioned into a teenager, she became quite independent. She never sought permission to visit her grandmother, and the Murungos did not mind. After all, spending time with grandma could only be good for their daughter. It was an excellent opportunity to learn the Kamba language and other traditions. And sure enough, Dorcas received more than the usual dose of Kamba cultural training for girls her age.

Dorcas also received much more knowledge of life than her parents realized.

During one of her visits to grandma, Dorcas met Steve Koelel, a teenager from Kangundo who was visiting an uncle in the Masii area. The two teenagers fell in love.

The bond between the teenagers was so intense it would have made William Shakespeare's story of Romeo and Juliet seem like a minor tragicomedy.

Luckily, it was in the modern era, and Juliet did not have to talk to Romeo from the ledge of an upstairs window. There was a more effective mode of communication: the cell phone.

Dorcas could not get enough of Romeo's photos and messages, nor could Romeo get enough of Juliet's poems transmitted electronically through cyberspace.

As far as Juliet was concerned, meeting Romeo had been the ultimate purpose of her life. There was nothing more important in her life. Period.

There were times when Juliet could not eat a full meal. She had been smitten by the love bug, which sometimes caused her nausea, which could only be healed when she received a message from Romeo.

* * *

Despite their training as medical doctors, the Murungos did not notice the effects of the infectious bug that had pierced their daughter's heart. So, when, on the night of June 16, 2009, Dorcas failed to return home from her grandmother's home, the Murungos went into a state of panic.

They made frantic telephone calls to Masii. They spoke to her grandmother, uncles, cousins, and other relatives. Nobody seemed to have any inkling of her whereabouts except one of her distant cousins, Christine, who said she had seen Dorcas with a boy heading towards Masii town two weeks earlier.

Panic turned into desperation. After trying everything humanly possible for about eight hours, the Murungos decided to do the unthinkable: They contacted the police.

The police had no record of Dorcas. They suggested they launch a search in all places where missing persons are typically found, including the morgue.

The idea of a search for their daughter in a morgue sent chills down the spines of the Murungos. However, the police handled the matter professionally to minimize the anxiety.

At around 3:00 a.m., Inspector Ochola entered the room where the couple had been asked to wait while the police conducted the search.

"I have some news for you," Inspector Ochola said.

"At least Dorcas is not in any of the morgues in the country. That is a good starting point, although I appreciate that that information does not solve anything," he added.

The Murungos simultaneously and audibly sighed a sigh of relief. But the news was neither good nor bad. The vacuum it still left was too much for Mrs. Murungo to bear. She could not help crying. She suddenly felt immeasurably close to her daughter Dorcas. It was as if Dorcas was an extension of her body.

"Please, Dorcas! Where are you? Please, please!" She cried.

"What shall we do now?" Murungo asked Inspector Ochola.

"We must speak to all her close friends as quickly as possible. If we do not get any leads, we may have to advertise in the newspapers or on radio or television to seek information from the public. But I recommend that we exhaust the first avenue before resorting to publicity. But you must give me the list of all her friends and their respective homes."

The request from Inspector Ochola was perfectly logical, but it revealed a certain hollowness in the Murungo family that they had not known before. They did not know the names of Dorcas' friends or their residences. It was a little embarrassing. So, they told the Inspector they would prepare the information and share it with the police at daybreak.

The search for Dorcas continued for three days. Just as the Murungos were preparing to head to the police station to discuss the newspaper and TV advertisements with Inspector Ochola, Jack Kangwana, Murungo's brother, telephoned Murungo. He said that Dorcas had been spotted by one of her schoolmates at Majengo, in Machakos, about one hour earlier. Murungo relayed the information to Inspector Achola. A manhunt was instituted immediately, involving the regular police and the detectives from the Special Branch.

Before dawn that day, Dorcas was discovered in a small rented shack in the company of Romeo. Apparently, Romeo had gone missing too. But he was from a single mother's home. A mother who did not have the time nor the remotest inclination to search for her son. They both lived a rough life in Majengo. She knew for sure Romeo would eventually show up. It was not the first time he had disappeared from home anyway.

The arrest of Romeo at Majengo caused quite a scene. Juliet could not let go of him. She could not comprehend what was wrong with the detectives who had nabbed Romeo and tied his hands with handcuffs. She screamed, causing people in the neighborhood to come to the scene in large numbers.

A New Perspective

As the commotion intensified, Inspector Ochola received the information. He prompted the Murungos. He quickly picked them up from their house, and the three sped to Majengo to retrieve Dorcas. The police car moved at high speed, with the siren blaring.

Upon arrival at the scene, they found detectives forcefully pushing Romeo into their car. Apparently, it took some explaining before the area residents allowed the detectives to apprehend Romeo. But the arrival of Inspector Ochola, adorned in full police uniform, immediately settled matters. Romeo was heaved into the back seat of a white saloon car.

Meanwhile, Dorcas, who was still crying loudly, noticed her parents. She sped towards her mother, who started crying too, and they fell into each other's arms in a daughter/mother embrace made in heaven.

"Why are they arresting Steve?" Dorcas cried as she was held tightly by her mother.

"Don't worry, dear. Everything will be fine?" Mrs. Murungo said. She did not say anything more in the next hour as the couple and their child were transported to the hospital. Inspector Ochola insisted that Dorcas undergo certain standard medical tests before proceeding home.

But to Dorcas, everything happening around her was the greatest devastation in her life.

* * *

The results of the medical tests came through at two different times. The anxiety as they awaited each test result was excruciating. It was like living multiple painful lifetimes.

When Mr. Murungo received a call from the doctor asking him to go to the hospital to receive the results of the first set of tests, he knew right away he was in for a rude shock.

Romeo had infected their daughter with a terrible STD, so the doctor said.

"Why? Why? Why? How could such a misfortune befall us?" Mrs. Murungo cried uncontrollably.

The devastation and emptiness that the news instilled in the heart of Mrs. Murungo were beyond description.

Mr. Murungo could not hide his disbelief and anguish either. For the first time in his life, he wondered what the purpose of life was. All along, he had reasoned that he was the most successful person in his peer group. But now, he wondered what even the word success really meant. The pain in his heart was too much.

But what was going on in Dorcas's mind and heart? And how would she take the information? That was the biggest question.

Three weeks later, the Murungos learned that Romeo had also impregnated Dorcas. This second piece of news was so devastating it almost drove the Murungos berserk. What had they done to deserve such cruel punishment? Mrs. Murungo asked her husband repeatedly.

The following week, the Murungo household was full of tears and sadness.

Subsequently, the Muringos came to terms with the situation. They could not turn back the clock. What had happened had happened. Looking back and wishing they had given their daughter better protection was futile.

They had to focus on the future and deal squarely with the new challenges.

* * *

Two years later, when the dust had settled and hearts had partially healed, Dorcas's bubbly demeanor disappeared. She had missed two years of school. Her story had appeared in the newspapers, and she had become the talk of the town for several months.

While Romeo received most of the public vitriol, Dorcas and her parents were not spared either. The world seemed to be full of unkind and vengeful-minded people. Some seemed to delight in the idea that a successful couple of professionals had suffered a big misfortune. Others even openly blamed the Murungos for not taking good care of their daughter and protecting her from an urban beast.

The family moved to Nairobi to escape it all, where they would be less conspicuous. And it was downhill for the Murungos and their daughter from that point on.

In the meantime, Romeo was taken to a juvenile remand home. The judge said that he should spend the next five years there, during which he would receive both physical and psychological treatment.

All this time, Dorcas lived a horrendous life of extreme introversion. Her feelings mutated from extreme betrayal to confusion. Something precious had been extricated from her tender young life by Romeo and by society at large. She could not bring her mind to comprehend what was going on in her life.

The miscarriage had not helped. If anything, it had made the psychological pain even more excruciating. She had even contemplated suicide to remove the heavy burdens from her shoulders once and for all. But the love she received from her mother and grandmother was far too much to waste on a premature, self-imposed departure from this world.

* * *

But miracles do tend to happen in this world. That was Mrs. Murungo's conclusion. After two years of intense prayers and care for her daughter, life had somehow turned the corner. Dorcas had gained enough courage to go back to school. But this time, it had to be in a boarding school. Far, far, far away from the eyes of those who had witnessed and directly or indirectly caused her untold mental anguish.

Dorcas joined Majimbo Girls' Boarding School in western Kenya. On the day she arrived, she realized, to her great astonishment, that her face was familiar to most teachers. She had already acquired a certain label that she could not erase from her life, but months of introspection had hardened her. She was no longer going to be a victim.

* * *

One afternoon, while on the playing field, a classmate uttered derogatory words that Dorcas concluded were directed at her. Dorcas immediately attacked the girl, causing the girl serious facial injuries. The matter was reported to the School Principal, resulting in Dorcas's immediate expulsion.

The school principal told Dr. Murungo that the school had zero tolerance for violence, regardless of what triggered it.

Dorcas had become the violent one, and getting another school proved problematic. But somehow, her parents did not blame her for what had happened. They knew only too well what could have triggered her reaction, and they were not ready to add salt to injury by blaming her for her actions.

After one year of unsuccessfully searching for another school, the Murungos resolved to enroll Dorcas in a business college. There, she would be in the company of more mature adults and, most likely, further away from potential problems.

The decision to take Dorcas to college was wise. She quickly adapted to the new environment and made new friends who seemed genuinely interested in her companionship.

But something had grown in Dorcas's heart, gradually yearning to come out. She became an angry rebel. She sought out political agitation groups and made every effort to secure a leadership role in any group.

By her third year in college, she had become a serious organizer. She led demonstrations vigorously in pursuit of all manner of courses. She became a fierce anti-establishment figure. An activist per excellence. She was no longer under the control of her parents.

However, her bold stance on controversial issues rubbed several people in authority on the wrong side, and she became a marked person.

* * *

On December 15, 2016, while leading a demonstration campaigning against the proposed destruction of old trees to build a hospital in Nairobi, Dorcas went a notch too far. She carried a portable loudspeaker that she used to castigate and insult certain prominent politicians who were behind the project.

She was back in the news, this time in a hood in front of TV cameras, with her angry image beamed across the country for everyone to see, including her parents, the Murungos.

It was Police Encounter Part 2 for the Murungos, but the stakes were less ominous this time.

Through her parents' efforts, Dorcas was released on bail. Through the philanthropic efforts of NGOs that supported some of the causes she championed, Dorcas received a light sentence for her infractions: the option of one month in jail or a fine of KES 100,000/=. Her parents gladly paid the fine.

It was evident to the Murungos that their daughter had mutated into something beyond their wildest imaginations. But there was something soft beneath the harsh labels that Dorcas had acquired. This emerged when she met Dickson Msalame, the Administrator of an NGO Dorcas had interacted with.

Dickson was attracted to Dorcas by what he perceived as her sheer strength of character. Something about her seemed to fill a gap in his personality.

And in a moment of passion, Dorcas emptied all her heart to Dickson. Dickson understood fully. Right then and there, Dickson decided that Dorcas would be his life-long partner.

On her part, Dorcas had found a partner more valuable than the most precious jewel on earth. Someone with whom she could confide her thoughts without fear or regret. Dickson was the catharsis she had been looking for since her unfortunate encounter with Romeo.

Dickson married Dorcas in a private ceremony at Nairobi, attended by close relatives and friends.

Dorcas lives with Dickson in Nairobi to this day, but the events of her past life still linger over her head. There are things that she simply cannot erase from her being, no matter how hard she tries. The scars that she received as a young girl never seem to heal. She is grateful to God for the gift of a loving husband, but the lack of meaning in the world seems to cast a never-ending shadow in her heart.

Imprudent

THE SCHOOL REUNION ENDED UP becoming a traumatic experience. Whoever brought up the idea had not considered its full ramifications.

Some things are better left untouched, such as old-school memories.

** * **

In Paul Otuoma's mind, Little Joe, as they called him back in the day, was still the rumbustious little "fella" who cracked jokes at every turn. A darling of all housemates in the Luke Dormitory.

Paul was well geared up for a fresh round of laughter about the pranks that he, Little Joe, and Edward Wafula performed on several occasions in their final year in high school.

Paul laughed silently as he tossed back and forth in his memory the wild escapades he and Edward went to in the third year of secondary school. On one particular occasion, they had gone into the local trading center and had stolen two jars of local brew from a local distiller. To an outsider, that was a crime, but to Paul and Edward or Ted, as his classmates fondly called him, it was a study in pure adolescent guts. To cap it all, they had enjoyed the brew and had gone to school in a state of total inebriation. And like brave spies in a movie thriller, they had gotten away with it.

They had waited outside the dormitories until the lights were turned off, then clandestinely and quickly entered and slipped into their respective beds.

The smell of booze was only evident to students in close proximity but far enough from the dorm captain to cause any serious trouble. The three mischief-makers suffered pounding headaches the following morning—a good punishment for their misbehavior. But the episode remained a permanent feature of their personal stories of braggadocio. They thought of themselves as heroes. These were the stories that Paul expected to relive, with immense joy, at the school reunion later that day.

* * *

But, as Paul was to discover, history has a strange way of reliving itself. As he approached the school parking lot, he could sense that there were a lot of surprises in store. The different makes of cars in the parking lot were part of the story of life that was to unfold in different shapes and forms.

There were three top-of-the-range SUVs. There was a uniformed driver in one of them. There were about twenty standard sedans of different makes. About ten other cars had seen their better days. They were still seen on the road because of the kindness of the Kenya police, whose motto is "*Utumishi kwa wote*" (Service to all).

There were two motorcycles too, and one bicycle. What did this configuration indicate, Paul wondered? A statistician could draw a perfect histogram of the vehicles and cycles based on their respective prices or, more precisely, on their respective owners' monthly incomes.

Paul was not the last person to arrive for the function, so the configuration of vehicle types, colors, ages, and prices would definitely change as the day wore on.

Paul did not allow for other participants who may have come on foot or by taxi as he performed his mental statistical analysis. So, the mixture of personalities would be even more interesting than he could contemplate—something probably impossible to depict on a histogram.

* * *

As he entered the school hall, Paul was met with strange gazes from what appeared to be old men who had walked straight out of one of those old horror movies occasionally shown in his early days in high school. After making three steps into the hall, an old man with a walking stick tapped his shoulders and shouted:

"Paul! My brother. Where have you been for all those years? I could hardly recognize you. It was the gait that betrayed you, my brother. You walk exactly the same way you did in 1960," The old man said.

"Wait a minute. Is this Joe, the artist?" Paul responded, forcing a fake smile on his face.

"Are you nuts?" the old man responded.

"Look at me carefully. If you call me the artist again, I will fine you three rounds of beer?" The old man responded.

Who the toothless hell is this? Paul said silently in his mind. The old man had obviously indulged in alcohol several hours before the get-together. He might have been mistaking Paul for somebody else.

"Look at him. The same old pretentious self." The old man added, forcing a loud artificial laugh to disguise his agony for not being recognized by an old friend. As he opened his mouth in "laughter," the missing molars were an unbearable sight for Paul.

"OK! Let me refresh your memory, brother," the old man said.

"Remember, *busaa ya bure* (free local brew)?" The old man added.

"You cannot be serious. Don't tell me I am talking to my great friend Ted?" Paul said, once again, forcing a smile on his face but wishing like hell that the conversation with the drunken old man would end immediately.

"Give this man two beers immediately," the old man said, pointing to an invisible waiter.

"How could you not have remembered me, my brother?" The old man said.

"You have changed so much, man. What happened? You have become so old so quickly," Paul said spontaneously but immediately regretted making the remark.

"You are not a youngster, either," Ted retorted, pretending to laugh.

Paul felt the pinch under his gut. He reasoned that he had been too quick to judge. He promised himself to exercise utmost restraint as he mingled with the other old schoolmates. He even started worrying that he, too, had become an old-looking geezer.

"Look! Let me say hi to Charles over there. I will be back in a minute."

Paul started wishing he had declined the invitation to the reunion. Everyone in the room looked so old. If that was a mirror image of himself, he had already reached the sunset years of his life without noticing.

He approached three old men who were talking in low tones.

"Hi, Charles!" Paul said gleefully.

Each of the three men looked sideways as if Paul was addressing somebody else who was not part of the group.

"Glad to meet you, Paul. It's Peter from 3M, remember?" One of the gentlemen said, extending a hand to greet Paul.

"Ohh! Pete. How could I have missed you? Sorry! You look so much like Charles. My sincere apologies," Paul said, regretting the comments immensely, but they had already come out of his mouth, and there was nothing he could do about it.

Everyone in the school hated Charles because he was the worst bully ever. So, mistaking Peter for him was tantamount to sacrilege.

"Tom, I am part of Peter's security detail," said the second man, extending his hand to greet Paul.

"Me too," said the third man.

It became apparent that Peter had become a person of immense means over the years. He was definitely the owner of one of the big SUVs parked outside the hall.

How did the brat get into all that money, yet he was always last in class? Paul wondered silently.

"What are you up to nowadays?" Paul asked Peter.

"I am in the import and export business. Have been doing it for donkey's years now," Peter responded.

"How about you?" Peter asked.

"I am in Sales. I am the Sales and Marketing Director of Timbuktu Hotels," Paul responded.

"So, you are the people who have been giving my son problems. Just watch out. He will soon remove the carpet under your feet," Peter added.

"What do you mean?" Paul asked.

"I do not know how he does these things. He is partnering with the Hercules Group from the US. They are currently negotiating with Prion to take over the Kenya franchise of GGG Group. Timbuktu is a subsidiary of GGG, right?"

"Absolutely! I need to meet your son," Paul said. He did not mean a single iota of what he had just said. But the venom he was processing in his body had not settled before Peter flung what must have felt like the year's biggest blow.

"You will meet him, alright," Peter said almost sarcastically.

"It was nice meeting you guys," Paul said, smiling cheekily, and moved away from the three men.

Paul was becoming desperate for pleasantness for a change. But he was disappointed. Almost everyone he met was either old, too old, super old, or unrecognizable. It reminded him of old bad memories.

As he continued to walk through the crowd, Edward came hurriedly looking for him.

"What is it, Ted?" Paul asked politely.

"Paul, my brother. I need to speak to you urgently," Edward said.

What did Ted want to tell him urgently 40 years after they parted ways after graduating from high school, Paul wondered? At the same time, he did not want people to see him hobnobbing with this drunken Ted man for too long.

"What is it, Ted?" Paul asked.

"It is very serious and urgent, my brother. I need to speak to you privately," Ted said.

How odd things could get, Paul wondered silently.

"OK! We can go outside the hall briefly if you like?" Paul said politely.

Ted led the way. His head was pointed downwards to avoid eye contact with other people. His eyes were too red and could frighten someone. When they got outside, Ted started the dialogue with an unexpected sense of urgency.

"Thank you very much in advance for your kindness, my brother. I will never forget the old days when you and I worked as a team. Those are days that I have kept in my memory, my brother. Do not, even for a minute, think that I have forgotten," Ted said.

"I cannot forget, either," Paul said politely.

"Good. You see, my brother. My son married this girl from West Africa two months ago. These girls from West Africa are just trouble. Can you imagine I had to sell two of my cows just to meet the bride price? It was terrible, my brother."

"*Pole sana!* (I am so sorry). How can I help? Would you like me to assist in retrieving part of the dowry?" Paul said jokingly.

"No, no, no! It is very simple, my brother. You see, because we were good friends in the old days, I know you can help me. I just need a small loan of KShs 100,000/=. I promise I will pay it back in one week. Paul, did I ever cheat you when we were in Form 3?"

"Of course not; you never cheated me," Paul said quickly.

"But Ted, we have just met. I do not have KES 100,000/= handy anyway," Paul said.

It took Paul another thirty minutes to extricate himself from this awkward meeting. In fact, after the discussion with Ted, Paul had had enough of the reunion. He did not go back into the hall. He drove off quickly to avoid his old and boring classmates seeing him.

* * *

The whole episode had almost completely emptied Paul's soul. For the first time, the phenomenon of his rapidly advancing age hit him like lightning. A certain nauseating feeling engulfed him. Something he was unable to shake off. Why had he bothered to attend the reunion, he asked himself repeatedly.

As he got into his house, he went straight to the bathroom. His wife Angela asked him:

"How was the reunion? You seem to have come back quite early."

"It was fine. But you cannot believe how old and grumpy some of those guys have become," Paul responded.

Angela did not realize Paul was rushing to the bathroom to look at himself in the mirror. To compare himself with the images of his former schoolmates he had seen two hours earlier.

"Thank you!" he said.

"Who are you thanking?" Angela, who had just walked past the bathroom, asked.

"Oh! I was just talking to myself," Paul responded.

* * *

The reunion organizing committee had done a splendid job raising funds to meet the cost of snacks and drinks, thanks to the generosity of three old boys who had become exceedingly well-endowed. The primary beneficiary of the generosity was none other than Ted. He drank different alcohol types to his heart's content on that day. He was the last person to leave. He had utterly embarrassed himself with drunkenness and devilish laughter at almost every instance. He had become a pathetic human being.

As he left the party, he put two bottles of whiskey into the outside pockets of his oversized jacket - a jacket that had last encountered the iron box in prehistoric times.

One of the old boys seemed to encourage him to carry the bottles of whiskey, perhaps out of pity or secretly out of a morbid desire for the old man to drink himself to the grave and cease to be a nuisance to the good people of this world. The old boy also arranged for a taxi to take Ted home, which turned out to be in one of the big slums of Nairobi.

* * *

But what had happened to Ted, many in the reunion had wondered.

* * *

Edward Wasike was born in 1954. He came from a middle-class family. He attended elite private primary schools. He performed well in his exams and joined a private boarding school for his secondary education.

While in high school, he got into bad company. He started imbibing alcohol, smoking cigarettes, and occasionally experimenting with marijuana through peer pressure. Because of this, he frequently ran into trouble with the school authorities. His academic performance also suffered tremendously.

His final grades in Form 4 were mediocre, so he was unable to continue his education. What made things worse was the turn in his parents' fortunes due to problems with the tax authorities.

Edward spent four years at home, doing almost nothing except frequently visiting the local shopping center to buy cigarettes or beg for alcohol from his friends. These two substances helped to dim his sense of purpose. He was constantly experiencing episodes of self-shame and loathed meeting his former schoolmates, except when he was inebriated.

Deep down in his heart, he knew that his drinking problem was a way of avoiding coming face to face with the reality of his situation. He was too afraid to change. He could not dare see his true, disastrous self. He had suffered a tremendous loss from his ceaseless imprudence.

Righteous

TO PHILLIP JOHNSON, THE PERSONAL transformation was almost predestined. But it had come at a huge personal risk. There was family, relatives, and many close friends to consider. They were dear to him. He was not sure that his new status would allow him to keep his friends. But he had one strong attribute going for him: bravery.

*   *   *

In 1965, a young boy emerged from his mother's womb on Christmas day. Those close to Anabel Chapman, Phillip Johnson's mother, considered the birth miraculous.

Phillipe Johnson's father, Greg Chapman, was a pastor in a local church in Sheffield. He had served as a chaplain in the army during the Second World War. His experience in the military had such a profound effect on him that he decided to devote his entire life to preaching the word of God after leaving the military.

This is the family that Phillipe Johnson was born into. His mother ensured that he went through a strict Christian upbringing: prayers before every meal, reading the Bible regularly, going to church every Sunday, and all other things that a good follower of Christianity was supposed to do. It was a solid upbringing, and the Chapman family was happy about it.

When Phillipe was ten, he was taken to a secular private school in Sheffield. This was a deliberate attempt to make him a well-rounded individual by ensuring he engaged with people from other walks of life. His parents felt that this would help solidify his faith in later life. It would give him a good worldview that would allow him to process his scripture knowledge effectively.

But sometimes, life unfolds in very unexpected ways.

* * *

During his fifth year in primary school, Phillipe started showing signs of rebellion against religion. He also started making friends with troublemakers in school. These were highly worrying signs for the Chapmans.

Phillipe's parents arranged periodic counseling sessions. The sessions did not seem to have the impact the parents were expecting.

Fortunately, Phillipe's grades at school remained reasonably good. He passed his primary school exams with good grades, which enabled him to gain admission to an excellent private boarding school on the outskirts of Sheffield.

Everything seemed to be going well until Phillipe reached his third year in high school. He could not keep his mind off girls and other vices. His religious faith took a back seat. He saw religion as a barrier to the pursuit of his desires, which he pursued with reckless abandon.

He got into trouble with the police three times during the school holidays. It was highly embarrassing to the pastor's family, but they could withstand the stress through prayer.

In 1984, Phillipe went utterly berserk. He was admitted to the hospital for psychiatric treatment. It turned out that he had been experimenting with hard drugs since his second year in high school. The doctor told his parents that if Phillipe did not refrain from taking hard drugs after six months of rehabilitation in the hospital, he could potentially descend into psychosis and never recover his normal brain functions.

The information about psychosis must have sent a serious message to Phillipe.

He had initially been in a state of denial, but on October 15, 1984, something he had never experienced before happened. He explained it as a supernatural transformation.

He summoned all his close family members, relatives, and friends to the hospital. And in a move that was almost unprecedented in the lives of all present, Phillipe talked from prepared notes, describing in detail all the things he had done in school that were contrary to the Christian faith.

In some instances, some people in the congregation shed tears in disbelief. Some of the things he had done were shameful. A few of them shameful in the extreme. But Phillipe was intent on a full release based on his supernatural encounter two days earlier.

He did not mind whether the congregation would like or hate him for his unspeakable deeds. His time for emotional release had come, and there was no holding back.

Nobody said a word after the confession.

His father said a prayer wishing him God's grace and mercy as he started his new journey of righteousness.

After that one-hour event, Phillipe became a changed man. He felt at peace with himself and with the world.

But deep inside his heart, he knew that he had caused pain and suffering to many people, particularly his parents. And that he would never be able to undo the damage. All that he could do was continually pray for the forgiveness of his sins.

Phillipe left the hospital a month later. He enrolled in a seminary in the southern part of Italy.

* * *

Phillipe has never left the seminary as he searches for the true meaning of life. He believes he has permanently joined a fraternity of the righteous.

Manipulator

IT REMAINED A MYSTERY TO the close associates of Joseph Motlanthe as to where he had suddenly picked up the strange behavior. Some believed it was something he had learned from his uncle in Johannesburg. Wherever he had picked it from, it was irritating to many and something that could ultimately land him in many difficult situations.

His uncle, a low-level administrator in the Mpumalanga region, was famous for pulling a gargantuan prank that almost got him fired. People from his village near Lekwa municipality had been complaining endlessly about the poor state of the roads in the area. It was as if nobody in the local government seemed to care.

But Motlanthe would not live it at the level of communal despair. He forged a letter from the office of the President.

The letter was addressed to all provincial administrators and other senior government officials. It alerted them that the President of the country was due to make an official visit to Lekwa and adjoining municipalities three weeks from the date of the letter.

The forged letter outlined in detail the route the President and his entourage would follow. Motlanthe's uncle made sure the route covered a large section of the road the people had complained about.

And in an almost miraculous activation of idle resources in the province, the problematic road was repaired in record time.

Just before the day the President was to visit, Motlanthe's uncle forged another letter postponing the visit to a new date that would be communicated later.

* * *

It took several days before the government officials in Lekwa discovered the letters were forgeries. But the matter was so embarrassing that no one wanted to pursue it vigorously. The provincial administration preferred to leave it at that. But to cover its tracks, the Head Office issued a vaguely worded letter promising to "annihilate" or "eat alive" anyone who forged government documents.

But the wonderful creativity and success of the prank were too sweet for the perpetrator to remain anonymous. So, Motlanthe's uncle cleverly fed information into the rumor mill that clearly identified him as the Albert Einstein of the prank.

Motlanthe's uncle became a marked man but relished in the overnight popularity for pulling off one of the biggest pranks in the history of mankind in Lekwa.

So, conjectures regarding the type of ethics that Motlanthe was absorbing from his periodic visits to his uncle's house were not too far off the mark.

* * *

On one occasion, when Motlanthe was in college, he waged a spirited campaign for the students in his class to boycott exams. The campaign was so effective that all the students in his class participated.

He even influenced the preparation of a memorandum of grievances that three students presented to the College Principal.

The gullible students did not know that behind the scenes, Motlanthe was communicating secretly with the school authorities and feeding them all manner of lies about the boycott ring leaders and what they were planning to do if their grievances were not addressed. One of the hints Motlanthe dropped was that the ring leaders would arrange to burn down the college administration block.

To Motlanthe's delight, the exams were postponed. Also, three students became unfortunate casualties of the saga. They were suspended for three weeks for engineering the boycott. The students were innocent, but their pleas fell on deaf ears. The evidence (false) gathered about their leading roles in the boycott was overwhelming. They had to face the music. They did not sit the exam, which had a devastating effect on their final grades that semester.

* * *

The deception was later discovered, but it was too late and embarrassing for anyone—the school authorities and the students—to do anything about it. But Motlanthe was marked for revenge at a more suitable date in the future.

Motlanthe later lost his front teeth in a bar brawl near the college. It was obvious that those teeth had to go as a substitute for a foul mouth, a slippery tongue, and his manipulative ways. He acquired the label snitch.

* * *

Motlanthe never stopped regretting what he had done to the other students. His sense of guilt and lack of an avenue to make amends have created a hollowness in his psyche that is indelibly written on his face. At the age of 40, he looks 60. A yawning gaping hole in his soul can be seen by anyone who talks to him for even five minutes.

CHAPTER 3

A Perspective on Archetypes

"You have to be slightly uncomfortable with what you're doing, and you have to be able to try to find moments of newness."
—Jonathan Anderson

ON JANUARY 8, 2020, THE WORLD woke up to unexpected news. Prince Harry, the Duke of Sussex, and his wife, Meghan Markle, the Duchess of Sussex, had renounced their positions in the British monarchy and were headed for America to start a new life as independent ordinary citizens. Their withdrawal from duties in the British monarchy was dubbed Megxit, a portmanteau likening the event to Britain's exit from the European Union.

Many people worldwide were shocked by the news. This was an unprecedented break from tradition. One could only conjecture the utter shock and disbelief within the royal household in England.

The news from California fourteen months later, on March 7, 2021, came as another bombshell. Oprah Winfrey, the ultimate queen of talk show in America, had interviewed the estranged Prince and Princess. The couple had spilled beans about family struggles and racism in the royal palace since their marriage on May 19, 2018.[2]

Who would have thought such a highly regarded couple would be the victim of the dark side of labels?

The tabloids and TV stations were abuzz with news of the revelations. Interestingly, audiences in their motherland in England received their dose of the shock several hours after TV audiences in the Western hemisphere had already swallowed the intrigue and were ruminating over its ramifications. Reason: time zone difference.

Meghan had told Oprah Winfrey that her skin color had apparently caused a stir in the royal household, with a prominent member of the royal household having the affront of asking what the skin color of their unborn child, Archie, would be – a surreptitious indication of the royal family's concern about black blood mixing with white royal blood.

There were several other earth-shattering revelations. For example, the fact that the Princess had contemplated suicide because of loneliness and isolation in the royal household.

Also, the Prince disclosed that his brother and their father felt trapped in the royal family due to the extreme constraints placed on them by virtue of their positions in the monarchy.

The shenanigans in the palace had apparently caused the couple so much anguish they had decided to relinquish their positions in the royal household and live as private citizens. They had quickly made an exit from England and traveled to Canada.

While in Canada, they moved back and forth to California. It did not take long for them to find help from a friend as they searched for suitable accommodation in California. Apparently, the renowned African-American actor, producer, filmmaker, comedian, and scriptwriter Tyler Perry allowed them to use his palatial mansion in Hollywood, free of charge, as they looked for more permanent accommodation.[3]

Tyler Perry himself was in the news a few months earlier when he revealed that he was going through a mid-life crisis, having just split up from his girlfriend and mother of his only child. He had said:

"I'm 51, single, and wondering what the next chapter in my life will look like. Whatever it looks like, I'm going to walk with God, be the best father and man I can be, hold my head up high, and try to look my best doing it!!" Mr. Perry wrote in a post on his Instagram page.

In a world with so much sadness, please try and stay in the good!".[4]

A New Perspective

In mid-March 2021, it was reported in the press that Prince Harry had joined a San Francisco-based start-up, Better Up Inc., as Chief Impact Officer. The company provides employee coaching and mental health services.[5]

* * *

As far as contemporary history goes, the story of Prince Harry, the Duke of Sussex, and Meghan Markle, the Princess of Sussex, would have to be the most fascinating for historians.

But if we examine the story closely, we will notice that the question of identity is at its core. The royal family, a group of individuals born in England within families steeped in tradition, a tradition of immense privilege over other members of society, felt threatened that a free spirit within the royal household had engaged himself with an individual without a powerful enough label – a commoner and a half-caste. And they perceived this as a significant threat to the sustainability of the labels that had served the progeny of the royal household so well for so many years.

Ironically, Prince Harry's mother, Princess Diana, may have suffered the same loneliness and isolation during her short-lived life in the royal palace. Her estrangement from her husband, Prince Charles, was controversial due to the infidelity of the latter. But it was nothing compared to the storm she triggered from subsequent liaisons with Mohammed Dodi Fayed, the son of Mohamed Al-Fayed, owner of the Paris Ritz.

When the news first broke out, it was like a nuclear explosion. What made her story high-octane in specialness was that her estranged husband was the apparent heir to the throne upon the demise of the Queen of England, Queen Elizabeth. And what a stain to the monarchy it would have been if the former wife of the King of England was the wife of an Arab, with all the connotations that label carried in the contemporary world at the time.

But death does indeed have a way of solving certain labeling problems. The passing away of Diana and Dodi Fayed in a car accident in Paris on the night of August 31, 1997, dealt a death blow to any such risk, a somber outcome for the royal family and perhaps to many people in England who, in one way or another appropriated a certain value from their inherited association with the monarchy.

Mathew Angel of the Guardian reported it vividly.

"The news, as it seeped into public consciousness on a sleepy Sunday morning, stunned Britain and the world as no event has done since the assassination of President John F. Kennedy 34 years ago.

Though she held no official position, her life and death are likely to acquire the same iconic significance as Kennedy's. The candle has burned out; the legend will never die.

The effects may be overwhelming. It is possible that Diana, whose life nearly ended the British monarchy, might in death lead to its rehabilitation.

The royal story has suddenly been changed from farce to tragedy. As attention now refocuses on Prince William, the divisions that have tormented the royal family for the past few years may begin to heal."[6]

It is not hard to figure out the kind of life that Meghan is going through right now by virtue of a label that she will never shun, despite her spirited attempts, publicly or privately. She has been destined to live a life of high-octane labels. The best she can do is polish up her present labels so that they can synchronize well with her inherited labels and appropriate for herself incremental value in that process.

* * *

But the Princess of Sussex is much luckier than Priscilla Akinyi Mackintosh, whom we met earlier. Priscilla wrestled with labels from early childhood. Unfortunately, some of the labels defined the trajectory of her life. They also defined her very being during the temporary sojourn she would have as a citizen of this earth.

If the question was asked: Who is Priscilla Akinyi Mackintosh? The answer would have to be in terms of the labels she inherited when she emerged from her mother's womb. The labels ascribed to her as she grew up and the labels she deliberately acquired of her own volition.

Indeed, even when she departs from this earth, the labels will be immortalized in her eulogy and other written documents and images that she will leave behind.

The records will say that Priscilla Akinyi Mackintosh was a half-caste of African and Scottish descent, a student of Godfrey Ashcombe School in London, a student of Godfrey Ashcomb High School in Hampstead, a graduate of Ashcombe University, an environmentalist, a loving wife, and a mother. These and many other labels would constitute the alpha and omega of Priscilla's being.

Priscilla would bequeath some of her labels to future generations. She would not have much choice in it, nor would the inheritors of her labels.

We could classify Priscilla into one archetype, namely, observer. In other words, one whose primary predisposition is to observe the external world. One who exercises maximum restraint to avoid disturbing the normal flow of events.

Thomas Kamau, a resident of Makadara who hails from Kangema, a trouble-maker from a young age when he was a schoolboy, the *kihii* who grew into a responsible *mwanake* but whose schooling was hijacked by peer pressure from other schoolboys of bad behavior, who is a mason but has a penchant for following his successful former school-mates seeking favors, and so on. An individual who falls under the archetype, loser. Somebody, and there are many of these somebody's, who suffer from a deficiency of the drive to lead but are more prone to following others they perceive as more successful than them.

The archetype, Zombie, speaks for itself. This is an accolade that Salim Chokwe deserves for leading a life whose daily agenda was decided by others, especially his doting mother when he was a child. By allowing himself to be the puppet of others, he becomes an almost sensation-free human object that does not see life beyond the material things that have created an unparalleled sense of entitlement in a strange twist of the psyche. Salim is lazy, a mother's boy, an overgrown brat, and more. The attributes of the Zombie archetype will be challenging to remove from his very being.

But there are times when circumstances unfold in such a way that out of the sheer quest for survival, one develops character traits that define him in many positive ways. After suddenly becoming the victim of his father's misfortunes, Albert Saha becomes a self-driven, hard-working entrepreneur. A student of exceptional diligence, nominated by his teachers to assume leadership responsibilities as a young man in school. His self-drive earns him the admiration of other students at university. And it does not end there. He graduates with flying colors and gains recognition as an intelligent, ambitious mechanical engineer. His positive labels earn him a good position as the chief executive of a major firm. In sum, Albert falls into the leader archetype. One who sets an agenda for himself or others and influences others to follow him.

When Dorcas met her Romeo, she had, for all intents and purposes, fulfilled her life's dreams. But it was not to be. Her lover, one Steve Koelel, had other labels that had Dorcas known about; she would never have wanted to touch him with a ten-foot pole. But she was the ultimate victim of circumstances, ending up as a helpless young, pregnant schoolgirl suffering from a shameful ailment— circumstances that triggered a roller coaster of other events and demeaning labels from the outside world. And eventually turning her into a rebel in society. And to survive the harsh world, choosing to become a rebel seeking justice for other peoples' causes. In the process, acquiring multiple labels that put her squarely in the activist archetype.

But some deliberately make unwise decisions, never seeming to learn from their mistakes, and end up in the gutter. People like Edward Wasike, who came from a middle-class family background but, after falling into bad company in high school, never dug himself out of the hole of substance abuse. Eventually, becoming a pathetic-looking, good-for-nothing drunkard who was a shame to himself, his family, and his friends. A member of the archetype that we can only describe as imprudent. And there are many imprudent ones running around in different parts of the world.

And then there are those, such as Phillipe Johnson, who suddenly receive a spiritual awakening through a conspiracy of certain unusual life events and immediately change course to improve their lives. Individuals who, in most instances, become associated with a particular religious faith.

A faith that defines their entire life from the time of spiritual awakening - albeit an awakening tainted by a preceding history of debauchery. These are the righteous archetypes.

And then there are those who believe that life must be lived by manipulating events and other people. These people tend to be heartless and frequently pay the price for deliberately creating antisocial labels for others. Joseph Motlanthe is a perfect manifestation of this archetype, a manipulator.

* * *

Some labels and archetypes become impossible to discard after their acquisition. Indeed, it becomes even more dangerous to try to do so. For example, once you acquire the label member of the mafia family, you may have to live with it for the rest of your life unless you do not mind getting your jaws or knees broken, or even worse, having a small two-inch metallic object pass through your left ear and out your right, or more commonly such an object going through your forehead and through your cortex. And, if lucky, you could get a few headbutts that would remind you of the importance of familial ties.

It is easy for most people to see this stickiness of the label through the metaphor of the mafia family, but the truth is that there are innumerable such families in everyone's life. If you are honest with yourself, you can count at least three such families you belong to and that you dare not even contemplate exiting.

At times, an inherited label becomes a source of untold spontaneous danger. This happened with horrid outcomes in the democratic republic of Rwanda in April 1994. If you lived in a neighborhood dominated by people carrying the label Hutu, but you happened to have inherited the label Tutsi at your time of birth, then your life instantly came on the line.

Many unlucky Tutsi-labeled people were seriously outnumbered, and there was nowhere to hide. They perished by virtue of the labels they acquired at birth. The skeletons of some of those people are preserved in the Nyamata Genocide Memorial Center in Kigali, Rwanda. The skeletons are a constant reminder of the brutality people can unleash on others due to hatred of a label associated with their victims.[7]

There may be many other labels and archetypes in human life. This tells us that what we become in life is essentially a function of the labels we acquire as we go about the business of life.

The following extract from the March 26[th,] 2021 publication of The Sun, a popular British tabloid, is instructive:

"The Duke and Duchess, who have set up home in California, have been linked to A-listers, including George Clooney and the Obamas.

Writing in the Guardian, Barbara Ellen said that the couple's chances of being accepted into Hollywood's elite have diminished since airing their grievances about the Palace to Oprah.

Ellen wrote: "Considering where Meghan and Prince Harry wish to end up, are they blowing it up big-time?

*"Put it this way: has Michelle Obama ever sat on a TV sofa b****ing about her sister-in-law?"*

Ellen pointed out that "such behavior" is the "antithesis of how the mega-rich, uber-influential, notoriously private elite conduct themselves."[8]

Prince Harry and Meghan Markle acquired new labels within a few months: mega-rich, uber-influential, notoriously private elite. And apparently, these labels did not live up to public expectations of secrecy, an unwritten code that Prince Harry and Princess Meghan Markle broke when they publicly spilled beans about their private lives in the royal household.

* * *

Labels and archetypes are at the core of who we are as people. Indeed, they are at the core of the hopelessness of some life events that trigger fundamental questions. Existentialists have been grappling with these questions for decades. Last time I checked, none of them seemed to have found an answer with overwhelming support and consensus.

The questions are: Who are we? Why are we here? What does it mean to be a human being? What does it even mean to be?

In the next chapter, we will explore how some prominent existentialists have tried to answer some of these questions. It will be interesting to note that their worldviews and ideas were shaped significantly by the labels they acquired in their lives.

PART III

*The Perspectives of
Existentialist Philosophers*

CHAPTER 4

What is Existentialism?

"You don't have to stay anywhere forever."
— *Neil Gaiman*

PHILOSOPHERS, OVER THE AGES, HAVE SPENT countless hours thinking and writing about the essence of human existence. And the jury is still out because none of them has been able to crack it once and for all.

Some philosophers have developed beautiful, well-thought-out ideas that have appealed to the human intellect. But that appeal must be qualified, going by the type of gabbled information that one encounters in philosophy literature from some existential philosophy icons. I say this with the greatest of respect because I fully appreciate how challenging it must have been for those philosophers to develop their ideas.

Whenever one reads the writings of philosophers, it is helpful to keep in mind that the vocabulary can sometimes seem verbose, as vividly and aptly described by Blanchard (2009) regarding how different philosophers would talk about the death of a certain major in the army:

- George Bernard Shaw would say, "The major was hanged."
- The British idealist Francis Bradley would say, "The major was killed."
- Bozenskey would say, "The major died."
- The German philosopher Emmanuel Kant would say, "The major's mortal existence reached its termination."
- The most verbose of them all, Georg Wilhelm Friedrich Hegel, would say, "A finite determination of infinity had been further determined by its own negation."[9]

We will explore what some renowned philosophers have said about the notion of human existence, or to put it in philosophers' parlance, "existentialism."

Georg Wilhelm Friedrich Hegel (1770 – 1831)

HEGEL'S LAST SPOKEN WORDS IRONICALLY reflected his writing style, which can be difficult to follow. That notwithstanding, he is renowned for his ideas, which were at the forefront of the existentialism movement.

He was fluent in several European languages, including Latin, Greek, and German. He was a voracious reader. He kept a systematic record of everything he read. He was a brilliant student, receiving prizes every year for being among the top five students until the ninth year and being the top student in his class from the 10th to the 18th year.[10]

Hegel was born in August 1770 in Stuttgart, Germany. His last words on his death bed on November 1831 were: "There was only one man who ever understood me, and even he didn't understand me."[11]

He started his upper-level education in 1788 in a seminary, the Protestant Theological Foundation, attached to the University of Tubingen. He was at the seminary during the early stages of the French Revolution (1789 – 1799). His philosophy influenced Karl Marx, a key historical figure whose ideas triggered the French Revolution and revolutions in other parts of the world.[12]

Hegel graduated in 1793. After a stint as a tutor to wealthy families in Bern and Frankfurt, he entered academia, initially as an unsalaried lecturer at the University of Jena in Jena, Thuringia, Germany, in 1881. He became a salaried lecturer six years later, in 1807.[13]

During his career at the University of Jena, he wrote one of his philosophy masterpieces, *The Phenomenology of Spirit*, published in 1807.[14] It is a book for philosophy diehards but a literary juggernaut for the literary faint-hearted, who should read it at the risk of losing their sanity.

Hegel continued his career in academia until his passing in 1831. He was not an existentialist, but as Wyatt (2021) stated, it is impossible to discuss the existentialist ideas of people like Soren Kierkegaard and Jean-Paul Sartre without referring to Hegel. That is because some of these existentialists came up with their ideas as rebuttals to Hegel's work.[15]

* * *

Hegel's main ideas on existentialism can be summarized as follows:

<u>Existence</u>

Existence is a dialectical process of thesis, antithesis, and synthesis. In other words, life is about two contradictory forces whose resolution mutates into a higher, more rational state.

Human history progresses in stages. Because each stage is imperfect, it triggers opposing ideas, which in turn triggers conflict and results in a resolution to a higher, more stable state. Hegel described this as the metamorphosis towards human consciousness, reason, and freedom. The term he used for the synthesis is "sublation."

According to Hegel, history is not merely a process of change but an upward spiral toward a condition of absolute knowledge.

<u>The Absolute</u>
According to Hegel:

"The absolute is...is approached by art AESTHETICALLY, in the beauty of material forms; it is conceived SYMBOLICALLY in religion, whose highest manifestation is "CHRISTIANITY," with its central symbol of the spirit-made-flesh; but philosophy is humanity's highest attainment because it comprehends the Absolute through REASON."[16]

Nothingness is the opposite of being, which synthesizes into becoming.

Soren Kierkegaard (1813-1855)

SOREN KIERKEGAARD IS OFTEN REGARDED as the father of existentialism.[17] He was a brilliant philosopher, with 22 books to his credit, three of which became popular in philosophy academic circles. The books were *Either/Or* (1843), *Fear and Trembling* (1843), and *The Sickness Unto Death* (1849).

He is remembered for his Christian edict that belief does not require objective rationalization but is instead something that requires a subjective leap of faith. Kierkegaard used the story of Abraham and Isaac in the Bible to illustrate this notion of faith.

God commanded Abraham to offer his son as a sacrifice. In a true act of faithfulness, Abraham obeyed God's command but was stopped by God in the nick of time before he could carry out the orders. Abraham's readiness to commit what a normal human being would amount to a heinous act of immeasurable proportions reflected total faith in God.[18]

Soren Kierkegaard was born to a wealthy family in Copenhagen, Denmark, in May 1813. He was the last born in a family of seven children. His early life was characteristically full of gloom and doom. By 22, all his siblings had died except his brother Peter. His father seemed to have a dark, sinful past, greatly affecting Kierkegaard's worldview. He died from a painful spinal disease in 1855 at 42.

From 1821 to 1830, he attended early school at the School of Civic Virtue in Klarebodeme. He subsequently joined the University of Copenhagen, where he studied theology. He graduated with a Master of Arts in October 1841.

Kierkegaard wrote extensively in journals and books, often using a pseudonym to disguise his authorship. Although his writings covered many subjects, he is best remembered for his philosophical works.

* * *

Kierkegaard attacked all aspects of modern human life. He attacked the rationalistic ideas propounded by Hegel.

He held that life is meaningless. Goals, love, desires, passions, and other human sentiments are empty manifestations of the human condition. He said that the only way out is defiance, namely, defiance against all life's horrors.

He said that life presents us with multiple choices, but we lack the understanding and wisdom to make the right choices.

If you marry, you will regret it; if you do not marry, you will also regret it; if you marry or do not marry, you will regret both; Laugh at the world's follies, you will regret it, weep over them, you will also regret that; laugh at the world's follies or weep over them, you will regret both; whether you laugh at the world's follies or weep over them, you will regret both.

Believe a woman, you will regret it; believe her not, you will also regret that; believe a woman or believe her not, you will regret both; whether you believe a woman or believe her not, you will regret both. Hang yourself, you will regret it; do not hang yourself, and you will also regret that; hang yourself or do not hang yourself, you will regret both; whether you hang yourself or do not hang yourself, you will regret both. This, gentlemen, is the sum and substance of all philosophy.[19]

Kierkegaard said that angst, or unhappiness, is written in the script of life. Further, life can only be understood backward but must be lived forward. He said one cannot be absolutely content even for half an hour. One comes into this world crying, without asking and departs without asking, either. In a nutshell, life is empty and meaningless.

According to Kierkegaard, the only way to live a meaningful life is to know Jesus Christ and live in complete surrender, completely detached from the world's material things. In other words, to have a leap of faith.

Fyodor Dostoevsky (1821 – 1881)

FYODOR DOSTOEVSKY WAS A PROLIFIC Russian writer whose works were and are still widely read in the Western world. His categorization as a philosopher is almost accidental. His literary works were not intended as philosophical works but rather as novels. One of his masterpieces is *Crime and Punishment*, an enormously exciting novel that is hard to put down. His ideas on existentialism are primarily contained in his book *Notes from the Underground*.

Fyodor Dostoevsky was born in Moscow, Russia, on November 11, 1821. He was the second child in a family of seven. His mother taught him basic reading and writing skills until 1834, when he joined a prestigious boarding school in Moscow. In May 1837, he joined St. Petersburg's military engineering college.

However, his heart was in literature. He loathed military studies, earning the nickname "unsociable crank." He graduated in 1843 and was hired as a field engineer in St. Petersburg. He resigned six months later and decided to devote his life to writing. His first published work was a novella, *Poor Folk*, which became very successful. This was followed by other works, such as *The Double* in 1846, *The Landlady* in 1847, *White Nights* in 1848, and *Netochka Nezvanova* in 1849.[20]

Dostoevsky was arrested in April 1849 for his affiliation with a literary discussion group that was deemed anti-establishment. He remained in detention for eight months. In 1857, while serving eight months of detention for his involvement with a group considered politically subversive, Dostoevsky and other prisoners were brought to the Semenovsky drill ground in St. Petersburg, where he was sentenced to death. However, the Tsar commuted the death sentence at the last minute. Dostoevsky was instead sent to prison for four years with hard labor. He relived the horror of that moment in his novel, *The Idiot*, published in 1869. He read widely and continued to write during his time in prison.

After exiting prison in 1854, Dostoevsky's writing career blossomed gradually, reaching high levels as he approached retirement. He wrote several masterpieces, including *Notes from the Underground*, published in 1864, *Crime and Punishment*, published in 1866; *The Possessed*, published in 1871; and *The Brothers Karamazov*, published in 1880.[21]

Dostoevsky died in January 1881 after suffering a pulmonary hemorrhage. His tombstone was inscribed with the words from the New Testament of the Bible, in the book of John, verse 12:

"Verily, verily, I say unto you, Except a corn of wheat fall into the ground and die, it abideth alone: but if it dies, it bringeth forth much fruit."

---

* * *

The existentialist themes in Dostoyevsky's works are primarily found in his novels *Notes from the Underground* (*1864*) and The Grand Inquisitor chapter of Brothers Karamazov (1880).

Notes from the Underground

Dostoevsky narrates the story of an unnamed civil servant who has quit his job and lives in a basement flat in Saint Petersburg, Russia. The civil servant turns inwards to examine and reflect on the underlying reasons for his predicament. The story goes deep into the author's perspective of the human condition and the meaning of life.

Some of the existentialist themes that emerge from the novel relate to action versus inaction, loneliness, isolation, and society; human nature; reason and rationality; and spite, pain, and suffering. [22]

The man engages in self-dialogue, hovering around his dilemma of action versus inaction. He believes he is intelligent but cannot act according to his rational thought. He seems to be gripped by his own sense of intelligence. He questions everything and cannot seem to come to a definite answer. [23]

Dostoevsky uses the underground man as a mirror of the torment humans endure as they gravitate within one small space that they don't seem to be able to extricate themselves from despite their human intelligence. [24]

The underground man lives a life of loneliness and isolation from society. He does not seem to have real friends in the community. He feels that he is more intelligent than other people and loathes them. He is not sure whether he rejects society or society rejects him. He lives a life characterized by a vicious cycle: voluntary withdrawal from society and rejection by society because of his awkward lifestyle. His mind vacillates between defiance and embarrassment. Sometimes, he feels he wants to be part of society. At others, he feels he needs to remain isolated. He cannot make up his mind. A situation reminiscent of what humanity undergoes daily. [25]

The underground man ponders over human nature. He is spiteful of himself and feels that human nature is spiteful and sick, too, just like himself. He believes that humanity is irrational and not wired to do good. He repeatedly compares humans to animals. He denigrates humans, saying they are merely evolved species from lower animals like apes. He expresses great pessimism about the human condition. [26]

The underground man vacillates over a life driven by logic, reason, and scientific facts. He reasons that man is irrational and that living a life based purely on reason and logic would be impractical. Further, humanity tends towards a life of subjectivity driven by emotions, where people can exercise free will and choice. However, his dialogue, once again, is full of contradictions. [27]

The underground man is full of spite for others and personal pain and suffering. He is full of malice for others in society. He is a sadist and a masochist. These character traits appear to be a way of revolting against rationality and his desire to live according to his free will. [28]

The Grand Inquisitor

The Grand Inquisitor is a chapter in Dostoyevsky's novel *Brothers Karamazov*. It is written as a poem centered around Satan's three temptations to Christ in the desert, as narrated in the New Testament in the book of Matthew, Chapter 4.

Jesus had spent 40 days in the desert when Satan tempted him as follows:

---

3 Now, when the tempter came to Him, he said, "If You are the Son of God, command that these stones become bread."

4 But He answered and said, "It is written, 'Man shall not live by bread alone, but by every word that proceeds from the mouth of God.'"

5 Then the devil took Him up into the holy city, set Him on the pinnacle of the temple, 6 and said to Him, "If You are the Son of God, throw Yourself down. For it is written:

'He shall give His angels charge over you,'
and,

'In their hands, they shall bear you up,

Lest you dash your foot against a stone.' "

7 Jesus said to him, "It is written again, 'You shall not [a]tempt the Lord your God.' "

8 Again, the devil took Him up on an exceedingly high mountain and showed Him all the kingdoms of the world and their glory.

9 And he said to Him, "All these things I will give You if You will fall down and worship me."

10 Then Jesus said to him, [b]"Away with you, Satan! For it is written, 'You shall worship the Lord your God, and Him only you shall serve.' "

"11 Then the devil left Him, and behold, angels, came and ministered to Him." (Mathew 4: 3-11)

In the poem, Dostoyevsky describes how Jesus Christ returned to earth in Spain during the Inquisition. The leader of the Grand Inquisition orders Jesus Christ's arrest. Christ is brought before the Inquisition, during which the Grand Inquisitor questions him about Satan's three temptations. Jesus remains silent throughout the trial.

On the other hand, the Grand Inquisitor accuses Jesus and finds him guilty of causing suffering to humanity for having given Satan the wrong answers.

In particular, by refusing to turn stones into bread or throwing himself from the temple's pinnacle, he denied humanity evidence of a miracle that would have made humans believe in God. Instead, he condemned humanity to a life of doubt and the burden of free will, except for a few in the church who were strong enough to avoid earthly comforts and maintain their religious faith.

The Inquisitor states that the church performs Satan's work in its quest to find the best for humanity by offering ways of avoiding suffering and promoting stability within the church.

At the end of the Inquisition, Christ walks up to the Inquisitor and kisses him on his dry lips, symbolizing his unconditional love, unrelenting faith, altruism, and forgiveness through ACTION, despite the rational skepticism and doubt of the Grand Inquisitor.[29]

Miguel de Unamuno y Jugo (1864 – 1936)

LIKE MANY OTHER PHILOSOPHERS, Miguel de Unamuno y Jogo's major preoccupation was not philosophy. He wrote novels, plays, and poems. He loved paper folding. He coined the term "cosmetology," the art of paper folding. During his adult years, Unamuno was a controversial figure. He became a political dissident and, in 1914, was forced to leave Spain and go into exile in the Canary Islands. He returned to Spain in 1931 but apparently could not resist further brushes with the new authorities in Spain. He was placed under house arrest in 1936 and died two months later.[30]

Miguel de Unamuno y Jogo was born on September 29, 1864, in Bilbao, Spain. He studied at the Vizcaya Institute of Bilbao and later joined the University of Madrid in 1880. He earned a doctorate in philosophy in four years. Six years later, he was appointed Greek language and literature professor at the University of Salamanca.

* * *

His primary focus in existentialism was on the interactions between intellect and emotion and faith and reason. Some of his main ideas included spiritual anxiety that acts as a driving force in people's lives. He believed that life was tragic because of humanity's knowledge of ultimate death.

He was preoccupied with ideas around immortality and believed that much of human activity was an attempt to survive after death.

Martin Heidegger (1889-1976)

MARTIN HEIDEGGER IS CONSIDERED ONE of the most important German philosophers. One of his most significant philosophical works is *Being and Time*, published in 1927 at the age of 38. It is considered a seminal piece of work in existentialism.[31]

One of the giants of existentialism philosophy, Jean-Paul Sartre, once said, "Philosophy in the twentieth century without Heidegger was unthinkable and, for any philosopher writing after Being and Time, impossible."[32]

But even so, *Being and Time* is an almost incomprehensible piece of literature for honest non-academic mortals. It was the first of what Heidegger intended to be a two-volume work. However, he never published a second volume.[33]

I have an unclaimed prize offered to any of my friends who can read and explain any chapter of Being and Time to me in plain English. In my world, and with great respect, Heidegger is the arch-guru of obfuscation.

In 1915, Heidegger went through a personal spiritual crisis. He rejected Catholicism, the religion of his youth.[34]

Despite his prominence as a giant in philosophical circles, Heidegger's reputation was marred by his association with the Nazi Party in Germany.

He joined the party in 1933 and was accused of promoting Hitler's policies and the Nazi Party in his position as the Rector of Freiburg University. He started distancing himself from Nazi politics in 1934. Still, the damage to his personal image had already been done and remains a stain on his academic profile up to this day. [35]

Martin Heidegger was born on September 26, 1889, in Messkirch, southern Germany, and lived in the same area for virtually his entire life. He started his academic journey as a theology student at Freiburg University in 1909. Two years later, he switched to philosophy, and he earned a Ph.D. in philosophy in 1913.

* * *

Heidegger's existentialist philosophy is a rebellion against 16th-century philosophical ideas propounded by Rene Descartes that the world was, in essence, a duality of mind (consciousness) and the external world, or subject and object, or observer and observed. The mind is the entity in which humanity observes the external world and derives scientific axioms regarding how it operates.

According to Heidegger, such a duality was misplaced. Instead, he believed that we should think of the world in terms of our "being." In other words, one does not have a mind separate from the world. One is actually one complete "being." We start off as children and find ourselves in this world.[36]

Heidegger then continued to describe the different modes of our existence in this world. The core of his philosophical problem was to answer the question of what existence is. Or what is it to be? For example, as humans, we are full of anxiety in the face of our guaranteed death or finality, worried about our ultimate death (not being), death as the cancellation of all our possibilities. With this in mind, what is the meaning of life, He asked? He did not give an answer. He said that the finite nature of our lives is alarming. We find ourselves here, and shortly afterward, we are gone. [37]

He talked about the thrownness of our existence (i.e., we are thrown into the world; we simply find ourselves here or projected into the world, with certain given facts about ourselves). Existence is ongoing. We are evolving creatures. Heidegger said that we are continually projecting ourselves into the future, time. [38]

On alienation, Heidegger said we try to evade the reality of our anxiety. Sometimes, we alienate ourselves by burying ourselves in social activities. [39]

Karl Jaspers (1883 – 1969)

KARL JASPERS WAS A LUCID, down-to-earth character who, unlike his contemporary German philosophers, wrote beautiful, direct, and easy-to-understand prose. He was a non-conformist and greatly opposed authoritarianism.

Jaspers was born in February 1883 in Oldenburg, northern Germany, and lived to the age of 86.[40]

He was born into a middle-class family that gave him a good education in elite schools. He spent a lot of time outdoors enjoying the wonders of nature. [41,42]

In his early schooling at Altes Gymnasium in Oldenburg, the teachers divided the children into three groups. He vehemently refused to join any of the groups. Eventually, the teachers put him in his own group—a group of one.

Karl Jaspers went through school isolated from other students. He developed a breathing problem that persisted for many years. He thought he had tuberculosis and, therefore, spent most of his school life until graduation thinking that he was about to die.[43,44]

He married Gertrud Mayer in 1910, the daughter of a prominent Jewish family. Given the politics in Germany at the time, the marriage marked him out as a potential anti-establishment figure. This matter became problematic for him later in his life. [45,46,47]

He was admitted to the University of Heidelberg to study law but switched to medicine after only three semesters. He majored in psychiatry, later switching to philosophy almost by chance. He wrote his Ph.D. thesis on a subject that was more of phenomenological philosophy than psychiatry, and the university decided to grant him a Ph.D. in philosophy.

He joined the department of philosophy at the university. He remained there until the end of his career as a professor of philosophy. [48,49]

* * *

At the core of his philosophical ideas was the dignity of the individual, perhaps reflecting his background in psychiatry, plus his anti-system thinking. He believed that every person has the freedom to think for himself. And just like children, you will always return to yourself no matter your societal role. There is a core in every individual that remains, irrespective of age.[50, 51]

One of his existential philosophies, as articulated by Salamun (2006), can be summed up in the following quote:

"The experience of boundary situations like death, suffering, struggling, or guilt is an unavoidable condition of human existence. Experiencing and overcoming those situations in the right way provides a basic opportunity to realize the meaning of life."[52]

Another pertinent conception of Jasper's existential philosophy is that man is governed by reason. [53]

The other two planks of his existentialism are the realization of life through interpersonal communication and reason.

Jaspers believed that the ultimate object of human existence is to attain authenticity through deep self-awareness and self-consciousness.

Gabriel Marcel (1889 – 1973)

GABRIEL MARCEL DESERVES A BIG ACCOLADE for coining the term "existentialism." Although considered one of the prominent twentieth-century figures in philosophy, Gabriel Marcel's primary occupation was as a playwright, literary critic, and concert pianist. It is said that he was even somewhat surprised by the recognition that his philosophical works received.

Gabriel Marcel was a prolific writer. He wrote more than thirty plays and over a dozen books. Interestingly, he did not gain much recognition as a playwright and literary critic. He is remembered more for his contributions to philosophy. He did not like the label of existentialist. He preferred for his work to be described as the philosophy of existence. He was an atheist for many years but converted to Catholicism in 1929.[54]

Gabriel Marcel was born in Paris, France, on December 7, 1889. His mother died when he was four years old. He was brought up by his father and aunt (his mother's sister), who got married two years after his mother's death. [55]

Gabriel Marcel studied at the Sorbonne and obtained an MA in philosophy in 1910. He then worked for the Red Cross and became a secondary school teacher. Subsequently, Marcel worked for various journals as a drama critic.

He became popular for his public disagreements with the renowned scholar and philosopher Jean-Paul Sartre, another giant in existentialism. [56]

✳ ✳ ✳

The most prominent existentialist theme for which he is most remembered is the idea of human freedom.

Marcel argued that humans tend to gravitate toward defining themselves through their material possessions. And that through this objectivization based on material possessions, people lose their intrinsic freedom. He believed that the "idolatrous world of perverted possession must be abandoned if the true reality of humanity is to be reached." (Zuidema, 2021, p.285). He believed a person can only experience true freedom by extricating himself from egocentrism. In other words, they avoid actions driven simply by personal desires and engage with other free human beings to gain a fulfilling sense of freedom. [57,58]

Albert Camus (1913-1960)

ALBERT CAMUS WAS A FRENCH ALGERIAN philosopher who won the Nobel Prize in Literature in 1957. He was the second-youngest recipient of the prize in history. Camus loved football and swimming, which were his two childhood hobbies.

Albert Camus was born on November 7, 1913, in Mondovi, Algeria, in a poor family. His father was killed in battle during the First World War. He died when Camus was less than one year old. His mother and other relatives raised Camus in a poor neighborhood in Algiers. [59]

He earned a scholarship to study at a prestigious secondary school. In 1930, he was diagnosed with tuberculosis and had to stay in isolation with his uncle, Gustave Acault. During his stay with his uncle, he developed an interest in philosophy. He worked odd jobs on a part-time basis to survive.[60] Camus joined the University of Algiers in 1933. He earned a Bachelor of Arts degree in philosophy in 1936. [61]

Camus disliked government bureaucrats. Partly because of this, he joined mainstream politics in 1935 when he joined the French Communist Party (FCP). One year later, Camus joined the Algerian Communist Party (ACP).

He saw politics as the springboard to pursue his agenda of preserving human dignity. He was later expelled from the ACP for refusing to toe the party line. This event enhanced his dislike of bureaucrats and his quest for human dignity. In 1938, he started his career in journalism. In 1940, he landed a job as the editor-in-chief of *Paris-Soir*, based in Paris. While in Paris, he wrote some of his major works, including *The Stranger* and *The Myth of Sisyphus*. [62]

The outbreak of the Second World War in 1940 disrupted his literary career. He left for Algiers but later returned to Paris, where he continued his journalism career with tremendous gusto. He was to earn the Nobel Prize later, in 1957. [63]

Camus died in a car accident on January 4, 1960, at Villeblevin. [64]

✳ ✳ ✳

The philosophical works of Camus are interesting reading, even for non-academic philosophers. One of his famous philosophical questions from his book *The Myth of Sisyphus and Other Essays* is:

"There is but one truly serious philosophical problem, and that is suicide. Judging whether life is or is not worth living amounts to answering the fundamental question of philosophy. All the rest — whether or not the world has three dimensions, whether the mind has nine or twelve categories — comes afterward. These are games; one must first answer." [65, 66]

Camus articulated his existentialist thought in this book. He started with the following quote from Pindar:

"O my soul, do not aspire to immortal life
but exhaust the limits of the possible."

Right at the outset, he was trying to drive home the point that since we cannot live an immortal life, we should try our best to make the most of the finite time of our current existence on Earth. Camus argued that people commit suicide because they have failed to see the meaning of life amid the uselessness of daily agitation and suffering. [67]

The other key point by Camus was the absurdity of life. As we search for meaning, we find that we fall upon an impenetrable wall, and the universe does not provide us with answers to our most profound questions. "The universe is mute and irrational." He calls this phenomenon absurd because our search for meaning results in a certain emptiness. The universe does not provide any meaning. It is an exercise in futility. When you break the walls, you see an empty, meaningless wasteland. Life is a mechanical cycle without meaning. So, you can either embrace the absurdity of freedom or continue living it. Camus suggests that living the absurd life is worth living. [68]

Camus seeks to revolt against the absurd by facing it and wrestling and holding the absurdity by the horns. Choosing to keep living to rebel against the absurdity that causes suicide. [69]

Camus talks about absurd freedom. In other words, the freedom to live a life that recognizes that there is no afterlife. That life is finite. A life without the expectation of false liberty after death. Freedom to embrace the current finite existence that one has been given. Accordingly:

"The absurd man thus catches sight of a burning and frigid, transparent and limited universe in which nothing is possible but everything is given, and beyond which all is collapse and nothingness. He can then decide to accept such a universe and draw from it his strength, his refusal to hope, and the unyielding evidence of a life without consolation." [70]

Camus compares our life to the myth of Sisyphus. He considers Sisyphus as an absurd person. The person pushes a rock up a hill, but the rock rolls back just before reaching the top of the hill, and Sisyphus has to repeat the process over and over again *ad infinitum*.

In other words, life is full of repetition. We wake up in the morning, eat breakfast, go to work, return home, eat supper, sleep, wake up in the morning, eat breakfast, etc., in a continuous everyday cycle.

Sisyphus knows of the futility of his efforts, but he keeps on repeating the process over and over again. And this is psychological torture.

Camus suggests that happiness emerges when we recognize the absurdity of our existence and the opportunity to stretch ourselves to the limits. Further, we need to accept the gifts we have been given in this life and appreciate the preciousness of the limited time we have been given. In other words, we must take ownership of our fate.

Jean-Paul Sartre (1905-1980)

JEAN-PAUL SARTRE WAS THE BIGGEST name in the existentialist movement of the 20th Century. The Stanford Encyclopedia of Philosophy described him as "the father of Existentialist philosophy." [71]

Jean-Paul Sartre's towering figure in existentialism may have been mainly attributable to his entry into the philosophy academy just after the Second World War when people in his country, France, were exhausted from the war and were searching for meaning in life. He seemed to offer the answers and gained immense popularity for doing so. Unlike many other philosophers of his time, he lived out his existentialist ideas, albeit some of his behavior would stain his reputation to the end of his days.

His work tremendously influenced philosophy and other disciplines, including sociology and literature. He is also cited as one of the leading figures in the emergence of Marxism.[72]

The amount of literature that Jean-Paul generated during his 74-year lifetime was enormous. His most notable works include *Nausea* (1938), *Being and Nothingness* (1943), and *Existentialism and Humanism* (1946). In October 1964, he was awarded the Nobel Prize in Literature.[73]

The announcement issued by the Swedish stated that:

"This year, the Nobel Prize in Literature has been granted by the Swedish Academy to the French writer Jean-Paul Sartre for his work which, rich in ideas and filled with the spirit of freedom and the quest for truth, has exerted a far-reaching influence on our age."

But to everyone's surprise, he initially turned down the prize, claiming that he disliked official honors, adding that "a writer should not allow himself to be turned into an institution." Further, that accepting the prize would impact his writing.

Sartre provoked controversy in his writings, and the refusal of the Nobel Prize was just another provocation. In the end, the prize remained valid, as the Academy's rules did not allow it to be revoked.[74]

Jean-Paul Sartre was born in Paris, France, on June 21, 1905. He was the only child in the family of Jean-Baptiste Sartre, a navy captain, and Anne-Marie Schweitzer. At two, Sartre lost his father and was raised by his mother in his uncle's house in Meudon. His mother re-married when he was twelve. They moved to La Rochelle, a place where Sartre suffered bullying.

He was small and cross-eyed, which perhaps led to the unfortunate experience. He attended a private school in Paris, the Cours Hattemer.

He later joined the École Normale Supérieure, earning a Master of Arts degree in 1929. One of his legacies there was being a prankster per-excellence. After graduation, he pursued a career in teaching, except for a one-year stint in the army in 1939 during the Second World War. He also spent one year in prison starting in 1940.[75]

While at Ecole Normale, Sartre met Simone de Beauvoir, who became a lifelong companion and great philosopher in her own right.

* * *

Sartre's existentialist philosophy, in a nutshell, was captured in the announcement made by the Swedish Academy when they granted him the Nobel Prize in October 1964:

"Sartre's existentialism may be understood in the sense that the degree of happiness which an individual can hope to attain is governed by his willingness to take his stand in accordance with his ethos and to accept the consequences thereof; this is a more austere interpretation of a philosophy admirably expressed by Nobel's contemporary, Ralph Waldo Emerson: 'Nothing is at last sacred but the integrity of your own mind.'"[76]

Although his writings were not free of obfuscation like those of many philosophers, he became a household name in the Western world for advancing several interesting philosophical ideas.

Firstly, he said that things in life are stranger than they seem on the surface, which he referred to as the absurdity of the world. "To be Sartrean is to be aware of existence as it is when it has been stripped of any of the prejudices and stabilizing assumptions lent to us by our day-to-day routines."[77]

Secondly is the notion of freedom. Jean-Paul Sartre advanced the view that in realizing our freedom, we will encounter the anguish of our existence. This is because:

"... everything is terrifyingly possible because nothing has any pre-ordained, a God-given sense of purpose. Humans are just making it up as they go along and are free to cast aside the shackles at any moment." [78]

Thirdly, Sartre stated that we should not go about life in bad faith. He said:

"... we live in bad faith if we believe that things have to be done in a particular way and shut our eyes to other options." [79]

For example, in our choice of vocation, marriage partner, or even residence.

In *Being and Nothingness*, Sartre gives an example of a person who works as a waiter. He says that the man has convinced himself that he is a waiter, whereas he is a free creature and could as well be a fisherman, a soldier, or something else of his own free will. [80]

Fourthly, Sartre said that freedom is curtailed by money or capitalism for most people. In other words, they feel that they cannot exercise their free will and have to do certain things because they are motivated to earn money or not lose it. This idea was at the heart of Sartre's fierce criticism of capitalism, which, he said, limited humans from exercising their free will to live in other ways. This was his entry point to Marxism. Because of this, Sartre participated in many political demonstrations in Paris, agitating for freedom from capitalism. The establishment perceived him as a radical. The FBI kept a close eye on his activities. [81]

"Sartre is inspiring in his insistence that things do not have to be the way they are. He is hugely alive to our unfulfilled potential, as individuals and as a species. He urges us to accept the fluidity of existence and to create new institutions, habits, outlooks, and ideas. The admission that life does not have some preordained logic and is not inherently meaningful can be a source of immense relief when we feel oppressed by the weight of tradition and the status quo." [82]

Simone de Beauvoir (1908 – 1986)

IF THERE IS ONE PARTICULAR CHARACTER trait that Simone de Beauvoir will always be remembered for, it was her long-term romantic relationship with the Nobel Laureate Jean-Paul Sartre—and notably, the peculiar nature of that relationship. The two never married and preferred the "existential" freedom of an open relationship. Some may have considered it promiscuous, but the two saw it differently, with existentialism lenses.[83]

Simone de Beauvoir was also bi-sexual, a trait that created many controversies. In 1943, de Beauvoir was suspended from her teaching position, and her teaching license revoked for seducing a 17-year-old student, Natalie Sorokin. The license was later reinstated.[84]

Despite her shifting positions on some philosophical issues, Simone de Beauvoir was known for her force in intellect. She is most famous for her views on the feminine movement, triggered by her seminal work on femineity, *The Second Sex*, published in 1949. She advocated forcefully for the equality of men and women. [85,86]

Simone de Beauvoir was born in Paris on January 9, 1908. Her parents had wealthy roots and took her to a prestigious convent school. She had intended to become a Catholic nun but abandoned her faith in her teens and lived as an atheist for the rest of her life.

Simone de Beauvoir attended secondary school at Lycée Fenelon. In 1925, she joined Institut Catholique de Paris. Later, she joined the Sorbonne in 1928, earning a Master of Arts degree. After graduation, she pursued a teaching career, during which she wrote several essays and books, some of which touched on existentialism and existentialist feminism.[87]

* * *

Beauvoir extended Jean-Paul Sartre's existentialist philosophy to the spheres of social, political, ethical, and feminist philosophy. She asserted the central role of freedom in an individual's existence and argued that individual freedom was only possible in an environment where others were also free. In other words, there was equity among people in society.[88]

Paul Tillich (1886 – 1965)

PAUL TILLICH IS UNIQUE IN HIS articulation of existentialism from a Christian perspective, unlike his contemporary philosophers who proceeded from the standpoint that existence precedes essence. He is a highly regarded philosopher and theologian. He was born in Germany, studied there, and later emigrated to America, where he spent the rest of his life.

Paul Tillich was born on August 20, 1886, in Starzeddel, Germany, to a family of devout Christians. He spent his childhood in Schönfliess, a rural community where he enjoyed the natural forested surroundings. People there were deeply attached to their historical heritage and had a culture rooted in the Christian faith. This environment significantly shaped Tillich's philosophical outlook later in his life.[89]

He attended secondary school in Königsberg–Neumark and later in Berlin, an urban environment that seemed to offer him greater freedom of thought. However, that freedom did not erode his deep roots in Christianity.

As he continued his education, particularly at the University of Halle, Tillich became more interested in philosophy. He developed a keen interest in Schelling's philosophy of nature. Indeed, his doctoral dissertation centered on Schelling's work.[90]

He finished his doctorate at the University of Breslau in 1911. Shortly after that, he was ordained as a Lutheran cleric in Berlin. [91,92]

In September 1914, Tillich met Margarethe Wever and married her shortly thereafter. An interesting episode in Tillich's life was his decision in October of the same year to become a chaplain in the army during the First World War.

The experience in the army, with death and destruction all around him, completely changed his perspective on life. He even suffered from a nervous breakdown on three occasions. But even more unfortunate was Margarethe's extramarital affair in 1919, when Tillich returned from war. She got pregnant with another man, who happened to have been one of Tillich's best friends. Tillich and Margarethe divorced. [93,94,95]

After returning home from war, Tillich entered academia. He taught at Berlin, Marburg, Dresden, Leipzig, and Frankfurt universities and wrote extensively. While teaching at the University of Berlin, he met Hannah Werner-Gottschow at a fancy-dress party. They got married in March 1924.

Tillich had more than 100 publications to his credit in the 14 years between 1919 and 1933. He became a towering figure in theology and philosophy, a recognition that he enjoys up to this day. His most popular work is Systematic Theology, which he published in three volumes in 1951 and 1963. [96]

He left Germany in 1933 after being banned from holding any university teaching position due to his criticism of Hitler and the Nazi movement.

He emigrated to America and joined Union Theological Seminary in New York, where he taught until 1955. He then joined Harvard University. Upon reaching retirement age, he moved to the University of Chicago, where he remained until he died in 1965. [97]

* * *

Tillich believed that theology must resonate with reality in the contemporary world. He rejected the notion of supernaturalism or transcending the real, cultural, historical, and religious realm to interact directly with the supernatural. He firmly believed in cultural theology, the idea that religion must be rooted in culture. [98]

His existentialist views are cogently expressed in *Systematic Theology*. The ideas are immensely thought-provoking and may have even been misinterpreted by some as advocating atheism.[99]

In *Systematic Theology*, Tillich raises various existential questions and provides theological answers. He views philosophy as about asking questions and seeking answers, whereas theology proceeds from answers and then asks questions. To that extent, therefore, philosophy is a form of theology.

For Tillich, the existential and the religious are correlated. As he develops his ideas, Tillich argues that "God is to be thought of as Being itself.... God is not a thing, amongst other things. God is that reality that sustains being." [100]

Tillich did not engage in a discussion of the existence of God. He believed that such arguments were misplaced because inherent in such discussions was the presupposition that God is some form of an object amongst other objects.

He added that atheism was not possible because everyone, atheist or theist, has an ultimate concern and a yearning to understand life's real meaning. Even the theological ideas of God as an old man in the clouds are misleading because they objectify God as a thing. According to Tillich, Jesus embodies the idea of Christ, who embodies the idea of being—the figure who brings healing and salvation.

Paul Tillich talked about the idea of estrangement—dreaming innocence to existential reality—in other words, the sense of alienation we have about the gap between our existence as it is and how it ought to be. This gap is filled historically through the figure of Jesus Christ. Jesus Christ is the answer to estrangement.

Rudolf Bultmann (1884 – 1976)

RUDOLF BULTMANN WAS A POPULAR THEOLOGIAN. He was a professor of theology at the University of Marburg, Germany. He became famous for his ground-breaking work in which he tried to reconcile the mythology in the Bible with modern scientific-based reality. He offered a refreshing view of the kerygma that makes the Bible, particularly the New Testament (his area of specialization), relevant to answering modern man's existentialist questions. He averred that the literal translation and interpretation of the New Testament is misplaced. His approach was to demythologize the New Testament using an existential philosophy lens.

In the 1950s, he went on lecture tours in Britain and America. His works triggered tremendous debate within Christian theological circles worldwide.[101]

Rudolf Bultmann was born in Marburg, Germany, on August 20, 1884, in a family with deep Christian roots. His father was a Lutheran pastor, and his grandfather was a missionary.

In 1903, he joined the University of Tubingen to study theology.[102] The University had a strong history of innovative thought and theology. It was the *alma mater* of such leading intellectual figures as the astronomer Johannes Kepler, philosophers Friedrich Schelling and Friedrich Hegel, and the poet Friedrich Hölderlin.[103]

He completed his studies in 1912 and got a job as a lecturer at the University of Marburg. In 1921 he was appointed professor of New Testament. He remained in that position until his retirement in 1951.

He published his seminal work, *History of the Synoptic Tradition, in 1921.* In later years, he published several other books.

* * *

Bultmann was greatly influenced by his colleague, Martin Heidegger, who published his ground-breaking work on existentialist philosophy, *Being and Time*, in 1927. Bultmann saw Heidegger's existentialist ideas as greatly aligned with the theology of John and Paul in the New Testament. [104]

The two fundamental tenets of Bultmann's theology were that the early Christians had a mythological view of the world and that modern people had a scientific view. He suggested that the ideas around a three-storeyed world (the earth, the heavens where God and the angels reside, and hell in the underground inhabited by Satan), miracles, the devil, Satan, and the apocalypse during which the world as we know it will end in a cosmic catastrophe that will be followed by the judgment of all peoples some of whom will be consigned to hell for a life of everlasting torment and others will receive salvation and proceed to heaven for a life of eternal bliss, were all myths and should not be interpreted literally.

He said the myths could be traced back to Jewish and Gnostic myths, which were not believable or meaningful in the contemporary world. He stated that a blind acceptance of the myths would be irrational. [105,106]

To quote Bultmann:

"An important reason that intelligent men cannot accept these views is found in the fact of modern science as it shapes our thinking today for good or ill. A blind acceptance of the New Testament would, within this context, be irrational. Further more, to insist upon its acceptance as an article of faith would reduce the Christian faith to the level of human achievement. On this premise, he insists that we can no longer hold to the New Testament conception of the world, neither can we believe in spirits, whether good or evil.

Furthermore, the miracles of the New Testament have ceased to be miraculous, and the mythological eschatology is untenable. Equally strange and incomprehensible is what the New Testament says about the "Spirit" as a supernatural entity that can penetrate man and work within him. Biblical doctrines such as death as the punishment of sin, of atonement whereby man's guilt is expiated by the death of another who is sinless, and the resurrection of Jesus as an event whereby a supernatural power is released, are held to be meaningless today."[107]

Bultmann pointed out that the Bible contained philosophical materials relevant to modern man. He said that it was not a matter of eliminating the biblical myths. Instead, the myths required a fresh interpretation in order to appreciate the deeper truth "independent of the picture language and mythological thinking of earlier ages." [108]

Bultman stated that the philosophical existentialist life conceived by people like Heidegger, where humans are seen as having been thrown into the world as free agents, was confusing and frightening. It was a life where humans found themselves in situations they had not chosen, such as ethnicity, age, and family. Bultman said that such a life was not authentic. He noted that severing the mythological world had created even more distress, leaving humans with a life full of anxiety and sorrow.

Bultmann said that the Bible provides the formula for living an authentic life. Further, by demystifying the Bible, we can understand the right way of living without fear and anxiety. In other words, understanding the messages behind the myths.[109]

Bultmann said:

"Faith is the recognition of the activity of God in one's own life. Faith can only be attained existentially by submitting to the power of God exercising pressure upon me here and now. Faith means radical self-commitment to God in the expectation that everything will come from Him and nothing from ourselves." [110]

Bultmann was criticized by some theological scholars for approaching Christianity with preconceived existentialist ideas, most likely under the influence of the philosophies of Martin Heidegger and Soren Kierkegaard, but he received credit for his vigorous attempts to make Christianity intelligible and relevant to the modern science-driven man.[111]

Colin Wilson (1931 – 2013)

COLIN WILSON IS A PHILOSOPHER WITH an unusual background. He is associated with the notion of new existentialism.

Colin Wilson was a prolific writer. He wrote more than 100 books in a beautiful narrative style that was captivating to the reader. One person commented that he could even make the telephone directory very exciting. The book that propelled him to fame was *The Outsider*, published in 1956.

Colin Wilson was born in Leicester, UK, on June 26, 1931. He attended Gateway Secondary Technical School, where he showed great interest in the sciences. By the time Wilson left school at sixteen, he had significantly gravitated towards literature. He started writing essays and short plays. [112]

Colin Wilson subsequently worked as a laboratory assistant in his school. He left later to join the civil service, where he found the job boring. In autumn 1949, he left the civil service to join the Royal Air Force. But he did not last long there either. He pretended to be homosexual so that he could be dismissed.[113]

After leaving the Air Force, Wilson did several menial jobs. He also toured Europe before returning to Leicester in 1951. Wilson married and moved to London, but the marriage collapsed due to job instability. He never stuck to any job.

Colin Wilson wrote two books, but they did not do well. He went to France, but things did not work out well. He returned to Leicester, married again, and moved to London. Life was tough there, occasionally forcing him to live the life of a vagabond. While in that state of desperation, he turned inwards and decided to write about his experience in what was to catapult him into fame, *The Outsider*, published in 1956. [114]

* * *

The Outsider explored social alienation, creativity, and extreme mental states in the characters described in the works of existentialist philosophers such as Albert Camus, Jean-Paul Sartre, and Fyodor Dostoyevsky. Wilson explored the meaning and purpose of life that the world could not provide. He intimated that in modern times, the church could not adequately fill the gap.

Wilson had contemplated joining a monastery, but he felt it would have been a difficult experience given the worldly vices he could not give up. He also could not reconcile some Christian teachings in his mind. [115]

Unlike existentialists like Sartre, Wilson wanted to introduce the notion of altered states of consciousness or mystical experiences into existentialism—the high-intensity experiences that the early existentialists had left out in their articulation of the human condition. According to Wilson, such experiences dramatically revealed the essence and meaning of existence—something that he referred to as absurd good news.

The absurdity emanated from the fact that it was not really "new" news; it was already evident but had somehow been obscured by familiarity. He gave the example of a time when he wanted to commit suicide by swallowing hydrochloric acid but realized with almost supernatural lucidity that what he really wanted was more life, not cutting it short prematurely. [116]

Colin Wilson developed what he called new existentialism. He wrote about the idea of freedom, which we all like. But we only realize its importance when we lose it.

He discussed the idea of the indifference threshold—how we get so used to some things that we almost cease to appreciate their existence. We only realize that they are important in moments of crisis.

Colin Wilson extended ideas articulated by earlier existentialists that the "surest way for man to have a sense of his own being is to recognize the reality of his own death."

Wilson gave the example of Graham Greene, who wanted to kill himself using a revolver, but when he placed it on his head and pulled the trigger, and the bullet did not come out, the "world suddenly exploded in technicolor." He suddenly realized the vividness of life and the infinite possibilities that he had not seen when boredom had driven him to the point of suicide. He now wished to live even longer.

We all take things for granted and end up like Graham Greene Collin Wilson said. He described the idea of the robot, a labor-saving device that each of us has created that performs tasks for us so that we can get on with other things.

For example, when we learn to ride a bicycle, we no longer have to relearn the skill whenever we want to ride the bicycle. The same applies to many other things that we do in life. Wilson said that we need to learn to turn off the robot so that we can gain full realization of our being. He cited TS Elliot, who asked: "Where is the life we have lost in living?" The robot is what causes us to dislike a piece of music after hearing it multiple times. [117]

Wilson said that we need to periodically turn off the robot to live a more vital life by regaining some of what it has taken from our consciousness. [118]

PART IV

An Alternative View

CHAPTER 5

The Social Experiment

*"Every society gets the kind of criminal it deserves.
What is equally true is that every community gets
the kind of law enforcement it insists on."*
—Robert Kennedy

AFTER LIVING FOR MORE THAN 400 years as a normal human being, it was time for Binti Mwana Asha, the absolute ruler of the world, to update the Binti Mwana Mwana Asha Decree of December 2160, which read as follows:

"Henceforth, all members of the human race on planet Earth will endeavor to promote an open society. To that end, all physical and virtual borders of whatever nature will be eliminated.

This includes, but is not limited to, boundaries between countries and any physical manifestations of such boundaries. It includes barriers erected between communities of people, such as fences, walls, gates, doors, and door locks. It also includes computer passwords and computer firewalls.

Taxes, hitherto imposed by different countries that created and sustained artificial societal barriers, will be eliminated. The taxes will be replaced by one uniform value-added tax across the globe. The tax will ensure that people contribute equitably towards human development. In other words, taxation will be based on one's ability to spend, which will, in turn, be a function of one's income.

Additionally, there will be no speed limits for mobile contraptions of all types, no dress codes, patents, or title documents, and all forms of segregation will be eliminated. Entities created to sustain such segregation will be dissolved forthwith.

People's names will be altered to prevent association with any part of the world, as such associations are the breeding ground for discriminatory practices."[119]

Binti Mwana Asha was particularly concerned about people's identities. Despite her 2160 decree, people still carried too much historical baggage that limited their freedom and creativity. Almost all new ideas had been built on a foundation of old ideas, meaning the world had continued to develop on one uniform track for centuries.

ARCHETYPES OF HUMAN EXISTENCE

New ideas based on different worldviews were non-existent. Binti Mwana Asha was concerned that that situation would ultimately lead to the stagnation and annihilation of the warm-blooded human race. To address the concern, Binti Mwana Asha issued an edict to supplement her Decree of 2160. The edict read as follows:

To unleash the inherent creativity of the warm-blooded human race, the prior decree regarding personal names is hereby abolished.

Henceforth, warm-blooded humans born on planet Earth will not assume any name or other type of identification whatsoever. Every individual will enter the world as a free entity without association with any prior cultural tradition. Anyone who attempts to ascribe a descriptor of any sort to a child will be guilty of the crime of label ascription and will be instantly exterminated.

Additionally, and in further pursuit of this edict, studying human history and cultural studies will be strictly forbidden. All such programs currently in place in learning institutions will be eliminated forthwith. Learning institutions will adhere to the updated Binti Mwana Asha Science and Technology Curriculum without any deviation. The Central Command of the Binti Mwana Asha Surveillance Unit knows this edict and will monitor the activities of warm-blooded humans accordingly.

Everyone on Earth received the new edict instantaneously.

People's reactions were quick. The sentiments were varied:

"How will our children learn their culture?"

"We are moving into a world of heartless zombies."

"This edict will completely destroy competitiveness, which is at the heart of our education system."

"The edict will destroy a sense of accountability and cause a sharp increase in crime in a few years when the children become adults."

"I like the new edict. It will eliminate social segregation based on such retrogressive factors as race and color."

"Children will lose any sense of personal worth as they will be no different from robots."

"Does it mean that we can no longer worship our Gods?"

"Power, absolute power, corrupts. I cannot remember who said it, and I cannot even check it in history books. What has become of the world?"

People across the globe expressed many other sentiments. Most of the sentiments gravitated around the idea that newborn babies would grow into valueless zombies without any foundational ethics to guide them in their lives.

But there were others who subscribed to the Binti Mwana Asha's existentialist experiment. To some, this was just an extension of Binti Mwana Asha's never-ending quest to breathe life into robots.

This had started before she met and fell in love with Wanjala Patel, who later married her. That encounter had occurred after subjecting Wanjala Patel to torture in her laboratories in her Emotions Research Unit as she sought to isolate and develop computer code for human emotions such as contempt, despair, devotion, disgust, empathy, envy, fear, friendship, frustration, hatred, indignation, joy, kindness, pity, sadness, share, surprise, trust, and love. The experiments were still ongoing but had not yielded anything of value for her enterprise.

It was ironic that Binti Mwana Asha had succumbed to the human emotion of love and had become intimately involved with Wanjala Patel.

However, processing existentialist philosophy gave her new insights that spurred her into a new direction with plenty of promise. Even if the new initiative did not capture human emotions for transfer to inanimate objects such as robots, she was confident that she would gain invaluable insights into whether the raw human emotions were a direct function of acculturation.

Anecdotal evidence published in some prominent scientific journals suggested that such a link existed, but she looked down upon any inconclusive studies. The days of 95% confidence limits in scientific investigations in the 21st Century were long gone. Every laboratory test had to have an accuracy level of 99.9999999999%.

According to Binti Mwana Asha, the name science was synonymous with exactitude. There was no room for gaps that could create speculative thinking. Something had to be or not be. There were no two ways about it.

To Binti Mwana Asha, the edict would be the ultimate social experiment. Accordingly, she deployed the maximum resources to ensure the project's success.

* * *

The first child born after the edict was born in Naivasha, in the former geographical zone called Kenya. The boy's parents, Aisha Olbgeg and Steve Bhabujee, were elated. But they did not know what to do next, as any action that could be remotely perceived as following culture or tradition was prohibited. They were not even allowed to refer to him as their first child. He had no name. They had no choice but to just let the child be.

The couple was left with an excruciating mental void, but they had to get used to it for their own good.

Meanwhile, Ludwig Wamalwa, Head of the Surveillance Unit in the Binti Mwana Asha Central Command, had picked up the murmurings by the populace. He shared the information with Binti Mwana Asha.

Binti Mwana could not have any of it. But because of the pervasiveness of the sentiments, she became concerned that the issue could trigger a revolution.

Even if she had the capacity to quash any such rebellion, she did not want to risk it because of the potential multiplier effects on a useful human feeling that the Laboratory had isolated as a critical ingredient in human productivity, namely morale.

Accordingly, Binti Mwana Asha issued an Addendum to The Edict clarifying that to minimize the trauma on the part of fathers and mothers of newly born children, all such children would be transferred to a specially built facility in the Andromeda galaxy, the Andromeda Child Care Unit, where they would be taken care of by modern state-of-the-science robots that had all the human traits, including seamless smooth locomotion. The only human attributes the robots did not have were feelings. Still, the robots could simulate such behavior based on special algorithms built to facilitate interaction with warm-blooded human beings.

The children in the Andromeda Galaxy would be trained using the most modern science and technology curricula using modern state-of-the-science facilities.

The first batch of 60 girls and 40 boys arrived in the Andromeda Childcare Unit on February 16, 3002.

* * *

The Binti Mwana Asha Research Team was meticulous in its planning. The Unit was developed to offer the children multiple devices and gadgets to exercise their muscles and minds.

* * *

After the first six months, Binti Mwana Asha found the reports from the Unit interesting and highly gratifying. At long last, her quest for deep insights into the human condition began to bear fruit.

The children acted without any inhibitions. Most of them were inquisitive to learn new things. Differences in their body anatomy did not seem to be a differentiating factor.

Then, something interesting started happening gradually. The children began re-grouping of their own volition. The ones with similar external bodily characteristics began playing together. The boys seemed to want to congregate together—the same with girls.

There appeared to be some camaraderie within each group. This particular phenomenon applied to most children. However, a few children could not fit into any group and seemed frustrated that other children looked down upon them. The Binti Mwana Asha researchers did not intervene. They wanted to see what would happen.

The groupings started mutating into serious coalitions where children began displaying signs of wanting to share things with their group members.

However, as the children grew older, the groups started exhibiting signs of competing against each other for resources within the Unit. Binti Mwana Asha researchers had deliberately limited the resources to mimic reality in the real world.

And then, to the researcher's surprise, some children started exhibiting leadership qualities. These children had more muscular physiques than others in their respective groups. They could be seen giving instructions to other group members in a language they had invented. And to the researchers' further consternation, the assumption of leadership was not dependent on gender. There were as many aspiring male group leaders as female group leaders.

* * *

A few weeks later, the most incredible things started happening. The children began exhibiting complex behavior. Children in one of the groups were seen conspiring to attack another group that seemed to be endowed with more resources.

Researchers were not surprised by the formation of the coalition but by the apparent distribution of tasks amongst the group members, presumably for maximum effect when the attack was executed.

The complexity of the behavior was getting into new territory. The researchers' predictive systems could no longer cope with the complexity of unfolding behavior.

Then the unthinkable happened. One of the groups attacked another group with unimaginable ferociousness. Group members had apparently assembled crude objects within the facility that they used to beat up their opponents. Two of the children in the opposing group were beaten to death.

The secret cameras watching over the kids showed an almost spontaneous attack. None of the kids showed any feelings of mercy. They were like little brutes out to eliminate their opponents and snatch the maximum resources held by the other group.

And even after the fighting was stopped, the children did not show any signs of remorse. If anything, the robots that restrained them from achieving their ends had become another enemy force that would have to be eliminated over time.

This alarming event sent shockwaves across the Binti Mwana Asha research community. The parents of the children who died in the brawl were not informed about it.

* * *

Another dynamic emerged within the community of children. When the other groups learned of the attack, their tempers flared. In another two days, the groups were plotting revenge against the attackers. And another level of complexity emerged. Not only were the counter–attacks being plotted by individual groups. This time, groups started working in concert, with group leaders engaging in dialogue.

Three weeks after the first brawl, the researchers woke up to what could only be described as total war within the entire community of children. The children who were not part of any group were the first casualties. Several other group members sustained injuries.

The social experiment was becoming extremely dangerous. Binti Mwana Asha had to do something about it. The children were divided into smaller groups and dispersed in different locations within the artificial colony where they could not contact each other.

Things calmed down for several months.

* * *

The division of labor amongst the children intensified. One particular specialization that surprised the researchers was that of guards to protect the group from potential enemies. This role was assumed primarily by children of the male gender. Female children seemed to gravitate to roles that required softer skills, such as maintaining an orderly living environment.

* * *

The researchers noticed that the children's desires as they grew older were simply to satisfy their basic instincts. There was no moral code within the community. The most important thing was achieving one's desires without any sense whatsoever of what it meant to the community.

However, with time, group members seemed to develop a code of conduct that each member was required to follow. For example, group members who caused a disturbance when other group members were resting at night were attacked by other group members.

When the children reached puberty, matters got entirely out of hand as competition for members of the opposite sex became a life-and-death affair.

However, the incident that sent shockwaves through the research center, reminiscent of the first brawl several years earlier, was an attack on robots.

Some teenagers had become concerned that some robots had become too close to members of the opposite sex. This was unacceptable. The robots had to go.

Controlling teenagers became a significant challenge. They had to be restrained with remote control devices to ensure they did not cause harm to the community.

It was clear that Binti Mwana Asha had inadvertently created communities of brutes.

* * *

When teenagers grew into adults, they literally mutated into dangerous robots. They became self-driven robots that acted in their own utmost self-interest, irrespective of the feelings of others in the community.

The common denominator amongst the new breed of human robots was competition. It was everyone for himself and everyone else to the mercy of the Binti Mwana Asha Emotions Research Unit. Everything humanly possible in the pursuit of individual happiness was fair game. There was no reference to anything other than the outcomes from previous acts.

Some human robots became keen observers; those who could not cope with barbarism became losers. Many of them became utterly heartless, like zombies. The strong ones became tyrannical leaders. Several human robots who were out for revenge became activists.

Others did not know what to do. They had lost the sense of direction and had become imprudent. Some had engaged in debauchery most of their adult lives but saw the virtue of righteousness as a self-preservation mechanism. They were the righteous ones. But some had become nasty schemers. They were the manipulators.

* * *

It became a horrible world. A world more horrible than Binti Mwana Asha had ever contemplated, even in her wildest imaginations. She had to do something before things could get completely out of hand.

The solution: establishing another separate unit in the Andromeda Galaxy where humans from the research unit could be transferred for acculturation, including extensive tutoring on human history. A place to give them firm roots in the historic world before they could be released back on Earth. A place where they could gain an understanding of mutual respect, cooperation, love for one another, and the true meaning of life, no matter how mundane, unscientific, and unbelievable that meaning might be. A meaning that would offer them hope beyond their immediate material environment—a place to tone down their competitive spirit and over-zealousness.

* * *

But it was too late for some communities. Some human robots in those communities simply could not accommodate anything in their intellect that did not conform to the science and technology knowledge they had accumulated since childhood. They did not desire any education on the meaning of life. Life to them was the here and now. They just had to do whatever was humanly possible to ensure sustenance in the most comfortable way possible, with minimal effort. That is what mattered. Anything that did not contribute towards their comforts of the here and now was meaningless. In any event, everyone else in the system was predisposed in the same way, and yielding even an iota of ground for another person to benefit was unthinkable. The purpose of life was to sustain the here and the now.

The value of their being was measured in terms of the power they wielded to sustain the here and now. It would be too late to wait for anything more. In any case, assuring the here and now would automatically take care of the future.

Binti Mwana Asha arranged for the identification of all such human robots. They were rounded up and eliminated.

* * *

After conducting the experiment for 100 years, Binti Mwana Asha shut down all the Emotions Research facilities in the Andromeda galaxy.

It is not clear what happened to the subjects of the social experiment who remained after the elimination of the nauseating, insensitive communities that were steeped in a "culture" of hard-core science and technology. Rumor has it that the individuals still inhabit the Andromeda Galaxy in special rehabilitation homes.

CHAPTER 6

A New Perspective

"There's no alternative to being yourself. Accept it, honor it, value it - and get on with it."
— Rasheed Ogunlaru

THE QUESTION THAT CROPS UP in one's mind when thinking about the existentialist questions we have considered in the preceding chapters is: "Why all the fuss about our existence? We are already here anyway, so why even bother to ask questions about our existence?" To professional philosophers, Rene Descartes probably uttered the most apt words to describe the situation:

"Cogito, ergo sum." (*I think; therefore, I am.*)

This three-word sentence is perhaps one of the most famous arguments in philosophy. It is typically referred to simply as the *Cogito*.

Rene Descartes made the statement in the context of knowledge acquisition, namely, how we can establish the certainty of our beliefs. He was trying to put forward the idea that in a world where we cannot be 100% sure about anything, there is at least one thing we cannot doubt: "the fact that we are doubting." And if we are doubting, then we must be thinking, and therefore we exist. The mere act of thinking is, at a minimum, enough proof of one's own existence without any other form of external evidence.

However, the *Cogito* still does not answer other fundamental existentialism questions: "What is the meaning of life? Why do we even exist?" But it is a good starting point for discussing our alternative views.

* * *

The answer to the existentialists who ask these sorts of questions is another question: "Why do you need to know the meaning of life? Isn't it enough to make the best of the cultures, traditions, and material resources bestowed on you to make the best of yourself during your short stay here on earth?"

If one was born in Ukraine, there is not much they can do to erase their Ukrainian heritage. It becomes part of their being. Ukraine is permanently written in the DNA of their psyche.

If they were sired by an English mother and a Mongolian father, their being would be permanently embossed with elements of English and Mongolian blood. It would be part of their being. If they were born left-handed, that too would be who they are—a leftie. If they were born to Christian parents, they would be Christian beings by default. Christianity would be part of their being. We can continue, on and on, with the labels.

* * *

And while I cannot argue with the Cogito, I can categorically state that I have had more powerful experiences that convinced me of my existence.

One example relates to an incident several years ago when I was a teenager. I had accompanied my father on a visit to my uncle's home. My father parked his car near the main entrance of the house. He walked out and left me in the car. He obviously had some secret knowledge about the place he did not share with me – but perhaps he did not need to.

It was a beautiful sunny day. After a few minutes of sitting idle in the car, I decided to get out and wait outside. The warmth and beautiful light emanating from the sun were several notches stronger than the Cogito in reminding me of my existence and giving me a small glimpse of the meaning of life and why I exist.

But that was not all. Something else happened that reminded me of my existence in no uncertain terms. Two vicious dogs suddenly emerged from nowhere. They were big, ferocious Alsatians.

They were barking like they had completely gone berserk. I had no time to navigate safely back into the car. My intestines shrunk as I gasped for air out of fright.

But my angels were by my side on that day. They gave me wings to climb onto the slightly slippery bonnet of the car.

Meanwhile, my uncle hurriedly exited the house to restrain the dogs. The whole incident probably lasted less than a minute. But in those 60 seconds, I gained solid and incontrovertible proof of my existence.

There are several other things that are undoubtedly stronger than the Cogito. For some people, it is the fear of speaking in public. Even daily mundane life events are powerful reminders of our existence and indicators of the meaning of life.

* * *

Several minutes ago, I drank a delicious cup of lemon tea. The deliciousness started even before I put a single drop of the tea in my mouth as I observed the hot steam rising from the cup and producing a subtle tea aroma. The manufacturer had obviously put something else in the tea, as the aroma was quite tantalizing. I touched the sides of the teacup. It was too hot, but precisely the kind of temperature I like. I momentarily wondered how our mouths accommodate such high temperatures and how our tongues simultaneously experience the sensation of taste when subjected to such high temperatures.

As I sipped the tea, I consciously made mental notes of what was happening in my mouth. There was lemon juice, notes of honey, and traces of sugar - all combined in a hot and smooth fluid that produced excitement in my taste glands. After a few seconds, I swallowed the tea and discovered afresh the smooth sensation of the delicious fluid flowing down my throat like a small stream heading to the minute estuaries of my inner body. If this was not evidence of my existence, then the existentialist questions regarding existence are meaningless.

* * *

Returning to the existentialists' quest for the meaning of life and related questions, there is perhaps an alternative, easy, and practical way of answering these questions.

Firstly, we must be honest with ourselves and admit that nobody has come up with a satisfactory, universally acceptable answer. Theologians and philosophers have given different answers, but none can claim to possess the absolute truth. And that is the plain truth, although many people in either of these camps may disagree and argue that their version of the truth is the ultimate truth.

Indeed, when all is said and done, the different versions of the truth can be described as beliefs. It is what the person believes in, not necessarily what is absolute truth. And if everyone was to be completely truthful, they would admit that their version of the truth was not the absolute truth, that there was an embedded element of doubt.

If we agree that this is a reasonable starting point, we can explore alternative ways of answering existential questions.

That does not suggest that the quests for meaning have been worthless or should cease. No. That is not the point. The point is that it is reasonable to seek alternative ways of finding answers.

* * *

The Binti Mwana Asha story metaphorically showed us what being human means. Simply put, it is hard to contemplate how one can live a decent life without an identity, a historical frame of reference, and a foundation in culture and traditions.

A life without an identity is the life of a zombie. One becomes a mere contraption that responds to different stimuli to fulfill human biological desires like a savage.

As we progress in life, the labels we acquire solidify our being as humans. They give us a reference point and a mirror to view ourselves and position ourselves for success in this competitive world.

* * *

As we emerge from our mothers' wombs, we automatically enter a highly competitive world. Darwinian rules of survival immediately take hold of us. Our responses to the external environment shape our chances of surviving the multiple competitive challenges of this world.

Fortunately, many people enter the world under the care of their parents. As time progresses, the parents deploy all the survival methods they have learned to ensure their child survives and achieves happiness.

* * *

The most powerful methods of survival are label-dependent. The labels we acquire determine our relative competitive position in the world. There are three distinct types of labels: inherited, assigned to us by others, and self-acquired through proactive action.

A little later, we will see that a preponderance of positive labels, acquired through proactive action, can be a significant differentiating factor that may enhance our chances of success.

* * *

The inherited labels are those we acquire by virtue of the space and time of our birth and the labels of the people who gave birth to us.

The second category of labels relates to labels that other people in the competitive environment give to us based on our conduct or their own selfish, competitive motives.

The third type of labels are the ones we acquire as we grow up based on our proactive actions. We acquire these labels by deliberately shaping our external competitive environment and our position in it—in other words, our life strategies.

For example, when we join a school and pursue math and science courses, these would ultimately enable us to become members of professions such as medicine, engineering, and the like. So, when we fulfill all the requirements of the discipline of our choice, we automatically acquire new labels, such as doctors and engineers.

The combination of all three types of labels determines our being and the degree of our success as happy inhabitants of this Earth.

Accordingly, all the things done by different individuals in this world boil down to a dance of labels. Each individual seeks to enhance their own set of labels or labels of those closest to them in a particular space and time.

* * *

Let us revisit some of the characters we met earlier in the book. Priscilla Akinyi Mackintosh was born in Geoffrey Grey Maternity Hospital, London. That small space in the maternity ward, where she entered the world, would forever be part of her portfolio of labels. She was a Londoner by birth, whether she liked it or not.

What did it mean to be born in London in this competitive world? Perhaps not much for those who lived there, but the word London had certain powerful connotations for those who lived in British colonies. London was the center of global commerce and the seat of the most powerful colonial power. Priscilla may not have known or wished it, but her mere birth in London gave her certain competitive advantages. London was written in her very being.

Priscilla was born on June 25, 1963, a day forever marked in the DNA of her psyche. According to her parents' customs, that day would be remembered with great joy and celebration every year, particularly during her early childhood.

Coincidentally, that very day, another baby was born in East Finchley, London. That child would be known as George Michael, whose life would take a completely different trajectory but eventually become a towering figure in the global music industry. And by cosmic design, Priscilla's birthday would coincide with George Michael's. Both of them would indulge in a birthday party on the same day of the year every year as if linked in quantum entanglement. That amorphous link, too, would become part of Priscilla's being.

During the year of her birth, Priscilla's mother's ancestral homeland, Kenya, gained independence from the British colonial power. That event gave Priscilla's mother and Priscilla, by extension, tremendous pride—a big boost for her self-worth as an independent, free citizen of the world.

Priscilla would come to understand the true meaning of that freedom and independence much later. At that time, she would realize that she was inextricably linked, in a complex way, to millions of people in a distant land. She would learn that before her birth, she was partly an enemy of millions of inhabitants of Kenya who were agitating for freedom from people of her father's ancestry who had dominated them for many decades. So, even that remote event had given her freedom of some sort and that had become part of her being.

In time, she would learn that she had involuntarily earned the label of a former colonial master, even if only partially by virtue of her mother being one of the previously colonized.

Priscilla was also born of mixed descent. Later in her life, that seemingly simple label would weigh on her shoulders in ways that only her angels in heaven knew. It was an exceptionally powerful label in defining her being, marking her out from the rest of the people in her community in Hampstead.

Ironically, that label was a mark of tremendous beauty but also a source of immeasurable prejudice. It was a label that would create great hurt in her family. It was a big part of her being—a label she did not choose but one that she would have to live with for the rest of her life. It was a permanent label.

Six months after her birth, Akinyi became a Christian and acquired an additional name, Priscilla. Her parents timed her baptism to coincide with the birthday of Jesus Christ, whom Christians believe is the Son of God. That baptism into Christianity would be another significant label defining Akinyi's being.

As Priscilla grew up, she started acquiring other types of labels involuntarily. These are labels that were given to her by outsiders. What a charming little girl, some would say. Oh, she resembles her grandma, Jessica, others would say. I have never encountered such a naughty girl, yet others would say. How could she do that; she is a brat, others would say. Oh, she is so shy nowadays, others would say. She is a good student but a little taciturn, others would say.

Others would say, "She has proved to be a great environmental scientist—a big asset for our department."

During her life's journey, Priscilla would be photographed by her parents, siblings, relatives, friends, and others. These images would become permanent records of her physical features in different spaces and times. These images would give her fond memories of her nimble being as a physically evolving human being. The images would be special types of labels that would remind Priscilla of the agile, ever-evolving state of her being.

The list of such labels that Priscilla would acquire over time is almost endless. Some labels would be temporary, others semi-permanent, and others permanent. And all of them would constitute her being.

As a free spirit born in a free country, Priscilla also had the choice of polishing up some of her involuntarily acquired labels and even creating new ones of her choice. For example, in high school, she decided to study the sciences in order to become a scientist.

Priscilla proactively ensured she accomplished her goal of becoming a scientist by working hard in her academic studies. By focusing on her job and excelling in the projects she was assigned to, Priscilla earned other positive labels: team player, dexterous, diligent, and intelligent. All these labels became part of her being.

Even our classification of her under the archetype "Observer" became part of her being.

* * *

Thomas Kamau was born in a small village in Kangema, Kenya, over 6,000 miles from London, the birthplace of Pricilla Akinyi. As the saying goes, "You can take the boy from the village, but you cannot take the village out of the boy."

Kangema and his Kikuyu heritage are permanent labels Kamau acquired immediately after birth. Even the way he sounds when he speaks has something Kangema about it. (Some from Kangema have traveled to Akinyi's birthplace and tried exceedingly hard to speak with Akinyi's accent without much luck. The Kangema accent is stuck in their vocal codes for life).

Later in his life, people gave Kamau other labels, such as *kihii and mwanake* - labels deeply rooted in the Kikuyu people's traditions, with certain behavioral expectations associated with them. Through his actions, Kamau later acquired the labels rebel, smoker, mason, husband, father, and hanger-on. Even the archetype "loser" is one of the acquired labels. And there are many more. These labels and their interrelatedness with other objects and phenomena in space and time constitute Kamau's being.

* * *

Salim Chokwe arrived in this world as the only son of Halima, the youngest and favorite wife of a wealthy Swahili polygamous businessman in the coastal town of Malindi, Kenya – powerful inherited labels that defined the trajectory of his life. He lived a life of privilege most of his infancy, boyhood, and adolescence.

Along the way, Salim earned the labels "brat extraordinaire," "*Bwanangu Salim*," "*kifaru wa Malindi*," "*katumbo*," and others. His actions or inactions attracted yet other labels: docile, don't care, laid-back, obnoxious, manager, bachelor, and others. The archetype "zombie" captures the essence of several attributes embedded in some of the self-acquired labels. The complex web of things represented by these labels constitutes Salim as a human being.

* * *

Born in Nakuru, Kenya, in 1959, at the height of political agitation for independence in Kenya, as the eldest son of a prominent wheat, barley, maize, and potato farmer who died suddenly after the collapse of his farming enterprise, effectively leaving him to fend for his siblings, are some of the significant labels that defined Albert Saha.

Albert worked hard to wade through significant challenges. Others gave him the labels entrepreneurial and resilient. He earned the labels football team captain, debating club founder, good orator, student-union leader, mechanical engineer, production manager, managing director, golfer, choirmaster, and many others through deliberate proactive action. The archetype "leader" encapsulates many of the self-acquired labels. All these labels, their interrelatedness with other objects and phenomena in space and time, constitute Albert Saha's being.

* * *

Sometimes, a preponderance of inherited labels and labels given by others disproportionately impact what one becomes in life. The life of Dorcas is a classic example.

The daughter of successful professional doctors working in a provincial hospital in Machakos; a darling of her grandmother and namesake, Syombua, who loved her immensely and went out her way to teach her the Kamba culture; and the victim of an immoral youngster, Steve Kimalel. All these things crystallized into several labels, some of which would negatively define her painful life as a teenager and young adult.

But through strong actions, Dorcas would rebel fiercely against the society responsible for her predicaments. Indeed, she would acquire labels that would classify her as belonging to the "activist" archetype. Later, she would earn the label fiancée, wife, and mother. And once again, these labels and many others, their interrelatedness with other objects and phenomena in space and time, would converge to constitute her very being as a person.

Edward Wasike, on the other hand, is an example of someone who inherited labels that ought to have put him on the right trajectory in life. However, by making huge mistakes as a young man, he ended up earning himself labels that would ruin his entire life, almost irreparably: smoker, marijuana consumer, trouble-maker, and school dropout. His parents' financial misfortunes made things even worse for him.

Ultimately, Edward's biggest accolade was that of a drunkard, a subset of the "imprudent" archetype. An unfortunate manifestation of the interplay of multiple ill-fated labels, making Edward Wasike, or Ted, a label given to him earlier in his life in moments of fondness, a sad human being unable to cope with the reality of life and instead prefers to hide in inebriation.

* * *

Phillip Johnson's story demonstrates that despite the nature of inherited and other acquired labels, individuals can, through forceful, proactive action, make a major turnaround and live a new life free of the negative force associated with labels acquired previously. Granted, those earlier labels would still be written permanently in the DNA of their psyche. These individuals embrace decency and highly ethical conduct – attributes of the "righteous" archetype. This indicates that despite the complexity of the web of labels that define our being, there is the hope of disentangling ourselves and living a more meaningful life.

* * *

Some other people are predisposed to aggressively manipulating events for selfish ends. These are the schemers like Motlanthe. Often, they would have inherited and involuntarily earned various labels that would have put them in a favorable position in society. But they have no sense of the value of such labels.

Instead, they try to mimic other schemers who have come before them, sometimes with unfavorable consequences for themselves and others, earning toxic labels in the process. They are the manipulator "archetype." This is what defines their being.

* * *

Being, therefore, is the sum total of the permanent, semi-permanent, and temporary labels that we acquire in space and time by virtue of the place and timing of our birth, the external environment we grow up in, the culture and traditions we are immersed in, and the proactive actions we take to enhance our situation in the complex, dynamic, and competitive world we live in.

With this context in mind, we can find better meaning in life by leveraging inherited labels to our best advantage, vigorously polishing up labels given to us by others, and proactively seeking new, more refined value–adding labels. By doing this, we will live a progressively happier life, making the world a much better place to benefit our descendants.

BIBLIOGRAPHY

"Martin Heidegger." Encyclopædia Britannica.
     Encyclopædia Britannica, inc. Accessed March 16,
     2021. https://www.britannica.com/biography/Martin-
     Heidegger-German-philosopher.

"PHIL304: Existentialism, Topic: Unit 7: Simone De
     Beauvoir." Saylor Academy. Accessed March 19,
     2021.
     https://learn.saylor.org/course/view.php?id=30§ionid
     =299.

"PHILOSOPHY - Sartre." YouTube. The School of Life,
     November 7, 2014.
     https://www.youtube.com/watch?v=3bQsZxDQgzU
     &ab_channel=TheSchoolofLife.

"Rudolf Bultmann on Demythologising Scripture
     Explained." New Testament Explained. YouTube,
     January 24, 2021.
     https://www.youtube.com/watch?v=bISaqrcA8Oo&a
     b_channel=NewTestamentExplained.

"Simone De Beauvoir." Encyclopædia Britannica.
     Encyclopædia Britannica, inc. Accessed March 19,
     2021.

https://www.britannica.com/biography/Simone-de-Beauvoir.

"The Germans: Karl Jaspers." YouTube. YouTube, February 20, 2020. https://www.youtube.com/watch?v=tL4UuuZpAKU.

"The Grand Inquisitor | Dostoyevsky." YouTube. YouTube, May 28, 2019. https://www.youtube.com/watch?v=UduOywQZvZM.

Angel, M. (2012, August 31). From the archive, 1 SEPTEMBER 1997: Tragedy that struck at the nation's heart. Retrieved March 28, 2021, from https://www.theguardian.com/theguardian/2012/aug/31/tragedy-struck-nation-death-diana

Arnett, W.M., "Rudolf Bultmann's Existentialist Interpretation of The New Testament", 1963. https://place.asburyseminary.edu/cgi/viewcontent.cgi?article=2051&context=asburyjournal

Aronson, Ronald. "Albert Camus." Stanford Encyclopedia of Philosophy. Stanford University, April 10, 2017. https://plato.stanford.edu/entries/camus/.

Aronson, Ronald. "Albert Camus." Stanford Encyclopedia of Philosophy. Stanford University, April 10, 2017. https://plato.stanford.edu/entries/camus/.

Barrett, William, and Bryan Magee. "Heidegger & Modern Existentialism." YouTube. Philosophy Overdose, October 19, 2017. https://www.youtube.com/watch?v=bkQjj0vDHDk.

Blanshard, Brand. *On Philosophical Style*. South Bend, IN: St. Augustine's Press, 2009.

Bondarenko, Aleksandr. "Prominent Russians: Fyodor Dostoevsky." Fyodor Dostoevsky – Russiapedia Literature Prominent Russians. Russiapedia. Accessed March 15, 2021. https://russiapedia.rt.com/prominent-russians/literature/fyodor-dostoevsky/.

Bultmann, Rudolf, and Hans Werner Bartsch. *Kerygma and Myth: a Theological Debate*. London, UK: SPCK, 1972.

Camus, Albert, and Justin O'Brien. *The Myth of Sisyphus and Other Essays*. New York, NY: Vintage Books, 1955.

Cavanagh, N. (2021, March 26). Meghan Markle's 'DREAM of being friends with the Obamas And Clooneys is over.' Retrieved March 26, 2021, from https://www.thesun.co.uk/fabulous/14437658/meghan-markle-prince-harry-news-latest/

Chauhan, Yamini, Gloria Lotha, Amy Tikkanen, and Priscilla Young. "University of Tübingen." Encyclopædia Britannica. Encyclopædia Britannica, inc., 2020. https://www.britannica.com/topic/University-of-Tubingen.

Davies, Norman. *Europe: a History*. London, UK: The Bodley Head, 2014.

Desan, Wilfrid. "Jean-Paul Sartre." Encyclopædia Britannica. Encyclopædia Britannica, inc., 2021. https://www.britannica.com/biography/Jean-Paul-Sartre.

Flynn, Thomas. "Jean-Paul Sartre." Stanford Encyclopedia of Philosophy. Stanford University, December 5, 2011. https://plato.stanford.edu/entries/sartre/.

Friedrich, Hegel Georg Wilhelm, Peter Fuss, and John Dobbins. *The Phenomenology of Spirit*. Notre Dame, IN, University of Notre Dame Press, 2019.

Genocide Archive of Rwanda. (n.d.). Nyamata Memorial. Retrieved March 28, 2021, from https://genocidearchiverwanda.org.rw/index.php/Nyamata_Memorial

Hernandez, Jill Graper. "Gabriel Marcel (1889—1973)." Internet Encyclopedia of Philosophy. Accessed March 18, 2021. https://iep.utm.edu/marcel/#H1.

https://www.britannica.com/biography/Miguel-de-Unamuno

Kierkegaard, Søren. *Either - Or*. Princeton, NJ: Princeton Univ. Pr, 1987.

Kierkegaard, Soren. *Fear and Trembling*. New York, NY: Start Publishing LLC, 2018.

Lachman, Gary. "Colin Wilson's Ideas and Life by Gary Lachman." YouTube. Watkins Books, November 14, 2016. https://www.youtube.com/watch?v=-v7fMo0-i_g&ab_channel=watkinsbooks.

LitCharts. "Notes from Underground Themes." LitCharts. Accessed March 15, 2021. https://www.litcharts.com/lit/notes-from-underground/themes#:~:text=Thought%20vs.-,Action,the%20underground%20man's%20rambling%20thoughts.&text=This%20is%20because%2C%20quite%20simply,excessive%20intelligence%20basically%20cripples%20him.

Lotha, G., & Abhinav, V. (2020, December 27). Miguel de Unamuno. Retrieved March 31, 2021, from https://www.britannica.com/biography/Miguel-de-Unamuno

Manning, Russell, and Timothy Hull. "Paul Tillich by Russell Re Manning." YouTube. YouTube, June 25, 2012. https://www.youtube.com/watch?v=M_HcFLa0b1Q&ab_channel=TimelineTheologicalVideos.

Maryville University. (n.d.). Stages of human development: What it is & why it's important. Retrieved March 28, 2021, from https://online.maryville.edu/online-bachelors-degrees/human-development-and-family-studies/stages-of-human-development/

McDonald, McDonald. Internet Encyclopedia of Philosophy. Accessed March 14, 2021. https://iep.utm.edu/kierkega/.

Mucai, J. (2020). *A Day in the Year 3000*. Nairobi, Kenya.

Mussett, Shannon. Internet Encyclopedia of Philosophy. Accessed March 19, 2021. https://iep.utm.edu/beauvoir/#H1.

Österling, Anders. "The Nobel Prize in Literature 1964 ." NobelPrize.org. Swedish Academy. Accessed March 19, 2021. https://www.nobelprize.org/prizes/literature/1964/press-release/.

Perrin, N. "Rudolf Bultmann." Encyclopedia Britannica, August 16, 2020. https://www.britannica.com/biography/Rudolf-Bultmann.

Picheta, R. (2021, March 14). What we learned from Harry and MEGHAN'S explosive interview. Retrieved

March 28, 2021, from
https://edition.cnn.com/2021/03/08/uk/meghan-harry-
oprah-interview-recap-scli-gbr-intl/index.html

Remanning, Russell. "Paul Tillich by Russell Remanning."
YouTube. YouTube, June 25, 2012.
https://www.youtube.com/watch?v=M_HcFLa0b1Q
&ab_channel=TimelineTheologicalVideos.

Robichaux, A. (2021, March 23). Prince Harry, The Duke
of Sussex, joins BetterUp as chief Impact officer.
Retrieved March 28, 2021, from
https://www.betterup.com/en-
us/resources/blog/prince-harry-chief-impact-officer

Rohmann, Chris. *Dictionary of Important Ideas and
Thinkers*. London, UK: Arrow Books Ltd, 2017.

Salamun, Kurt. Salamun, Jaspers' Conceptions of the
Meaning of Life. Existenz, 2006.
https://www.existenz.us/volumes/Vol.1Salamun.html

Scharfstein, Ben-Ami. *The Philosophers: Their Lives and
Nature of Their Thought*. Oxford, UK: Blackwell,
1980.

Stassen, Manfred. *Martin Heidegger: Philosophical and
Political Writings*. New York: Continuum, 2003.

Thornhill, Chris, and Ronny Miron. "Karl Jaspers."
Stanford Encyclopedia of Philosophy. Stanford
University, July 17, 2018.
https://plato.stanford.edu/entries/jaspers/.

Thornhill, Chris, and Ronny Miron. "Karl Jaspers."
Stanford Encyclopedia of Philosophy. Stanford
University, July 17, 2018.
https://plato.stanford.edu/entries/jaspers/.

Tyler Perry: The US mogul who gave Meghan and Harry a home. (2021, March 08). Retrieved March 28, 2021, from https://www.bbc.com/news/world-us-canada-56320290

Unhjem, Arne. "Paul Tillich." Encyclopædia Britannica. Encyclopædia Britannica, inc., 2020. https://www.britannica.com/biography/Paul-Tillich.

Werkmeister, W. H. "An Introduction to Heidegger's 'Existential Philosophy.'" *Philosophy and Phenomenological Research* 2, no. 1 (1941): 79. https://doi.org/10.2307/2102674.

Wheeler, Michael. "Martin Heidegger." Stanford Encyclopedia of Philosophy. Stanford University, October 12, 2011. https://plato.stanford.edu/entries/heidegger/.

Wyatt, C S. Existential Primer: Georg W. F. Hegel. Accessed March 14, 2021. https://www.tameri.com/csw/exist/hegel.shtml.

Zuidema, S.U. "Gabriel Marcel: A Critique," *Philosophy Today* 4, no. 4 (Winter 1960)

NOTES

[1] Maryville University. (n.d.). Stages of human development: What it is & why it's important. Retrieved March 28, 2021, from https://online.maryville.edu/online-bachelors-degrees/human-development-and-family-studies/stages-of-human-development/

[2] Picheta, R. (2021, March 14). What we learned from Harry and MEGHAN'S explosive interview. Retrieved March 28, 2021, from https://edition.cnn.com/2021/03/08/uk/meghan-harry-oprah-interview-recap-scli-gbr-intl/index.html

[3] Tyler Perry: The US mogul who gave Meghan and Harry a home. (2021, March 08). Retrieved March 28, 2021, from https://www.bbc.com/news/world-us-canada-56320290

[4] Ibid

[5] Robichaux, A. (2021, March 23). Prince Harry, The Duke of SUSSEX joins BetterUp as chief Impact officer. Retrieved March 28, 2021, from https://www.betterup.com/en-us/resources/blog/prince-harry-chief-impact-officer

[6] Angel, M. (2012, August 31). From the archive, 1 SEPTEMBER 1997: Tragedy that struck at the

nation's heart. Retrieved March 28, 2021, from
https://www.theguardian.com/theguardian/2012/aug/
31/tragedy-struck-nation-death-diana

7 Genocide Archive of Rwanda. (n.d.). Nyamata Memorial.
Retrieved March 28, 2021, from
https://genocidearchiverwanda.org.rw/index.php/Nya
mata_Memorial

8 Cavanagh, N. (2021, March 26). Meghan Markle's
'DREAM of being friends with the Obamas And
Clooneys is over'. Retrieved March 26, 2021, from
https://www.thesun.co.uk/fabulous/14437658/megha
n-markle-prince-harry-news-latest/

9 Blanshard, Brand. *On Philosophical Style*. South Bend,
IN: St. Augustine's Press, 2009

10 Scharfstein, Ben-Ami. *The Philosophers: Their Lives
and Nature of Their Thought*. Oxford, UK:
Blackwell, 1980

11 Davies, Norman. *Europe: a History*. London, UK: The
Bodley Head, 2014

12 Wyatt, C S. Existential Primer: Georg W. F. Hegel.
Accessed March 14, 2021.
https://www.tameri.com/csw/exist/hegel.shtml

13 Ibid

14 Friedrich, Hegel Georg Wilhelm, Peter Fuss, and John
Dobbins. *The Phenomenology of Spirit*. Notre Dame,
IN: University of Notre Dame Press, 2019

15 Wyatt, C S. Existential Primer: Georg W. F. Hegel.
Accessed March 14, 2021.
https://www.tameri.com/csw/exist/hegel.shtml

16 Rohmann, Chris. *Dictionary of Important Ideas and
Thinkers*. London, UK: Arrow Books Ltd, 2017

17 McDonald, McDonald. Internet Encyclopedia of
   Philosophy. Accessed March 14, 2021.
   https://iep.utm.edu/kierkega/

18 Kierkegaard, Soren. *Fear and Trembling*. New York,
   NY: Start Publishing LLC, 2018

19 Kierkegaard, Søren. *Either - Or*. Princeton, NJ: Princeton
   Univ. Pr, 1987

20 Bondarenko, Aleksandr. "Prominent Russians: Fyodor
   Dostoevsky." Fyodor Dostoevsky – Russiapedia
   Literature Prominent Russians. Russiapedia.
   Accessed March 15, 2021.
   https://russiapedia.rt.com/prominent-
   russians/literature/fyodor-dostoevsky/

21 Ibid

22 LitCharts. "Notes from Underground Themes."
   LitCharts. Accessed March 15, 2021.
   https://www.litcharts.com/lit/notes-from-
   underground/themes#:~:text=Thought%20vs.-
   ,Action,the%20underground%20man's%20rambling
   %20thoughts.&text=This%20is%20because%2C%20
   quite%20simply,excessive%20intelligence%20basica
   lly%20cripples%20him

23 Ibid

24 Ibid

25 Ibid

26 Ibid

27 Ibid

28 Ibid

29 "The Grand Inquisitor | Dostoyevsky." YouTube.
   YouTube, May 28, 2019.
   https://www.youtube.com/watch?v=UduOywQZvZM

[30] Lotha, G., & Abhinav, V. (2020, December 27). Miguel de Unamuno. Retrieved March 31, 2021, from https://www.britannica.com/biography/Miguel-de-Unamuno

[31] Wheeler, Michael. "Martin Heidegger." Stanford Encyclopedia of Philosophy. Stanford University, October 12, 2011. https://plato.stanford.edu/entries/heidegger/

[32] Stassen, Manfred. *Martin Heidegger: Philosophical and Political Writings*. New York: Continuum, 2003

[33] Werkmeister, W. H. "An Introduction to Heidegger's 'Existential Philosophy.'" *Philosophy and Phenomenological Research* 2, no. 1 (1941): 79. https://doi.org/10.2307/2102674

[34] "Martin Heidegger." Encyclopædia Britannica. Encyclopædia Britannica, inc. Accessed March 16, 2021. https://www.britannica.com/biography/Martin-Heidegger-German-philosopher

[35] Wheeler, Michael. "Martin Heidegger." Stanford Encyclopedia of Philosophy. Stanford University, October 12, 2011. https://plato.stanford.edu/entries/heidegger/

[36] Barrett, William, and Bryan Magee. "Heidegger & Modern Existentialism." YouTube. Philosophy Overdose, October 19, 2017. https://www.youtube.com/watch?v=bkQjj0vDHDk

[37] Ibid

[38] Ibid

[39] Ibid

[40] Ibid

41 Thornhill, Chris, and Ronny Miron. "Karl Jaspers."
    Stanford Encyclopedia of Philosophy. Stanford
    University, July 17, 2018.
    https://plato.stanford.edu/entries/jaspers/
42 "The Germans: Karl Jaspers." YouTube. YouTube,
    February 20, 2020.
    https://www.youtube.com/watch?v=tL4UuuZpAKU
43 Thornhill, Chris, and Ronny Miron. "Karl Jaspers."
    Stanford Encyclopedia of Philosophy. Stanford
    University, July 17, 2018.
    https://plato.stanford.edu/entries/jaspers/
44 "The Germans: Karl Jaspers." YouTube. YouTube,
    February 20, 2020.
    https://www.youtube.com/watch?v=tL4UuuZpAKU
45 Salamun, Kurt. Salamun, Jaspers' Conceptions of the
    Meaning of Life. Existenz, 2006.
    https://www.existenz.us/volumes/Vol.1Salamun.html
46 Thornhill, Chris, and Ronny Miron. "Karl Jaspers."
    Stanford Encyclopedia of Philosophy. Stanford
    University, July 17, 2018.
    https://plato.stanford.edu/entries/jaspers/
47 "The Germans: Karl Jaspers." YouTube. YouTube,
    February 20, 2020.
    https://www.youtube.com/watch?v=tL4UuuZpAKU
48 Thornhill, Chris, and Ronny Miron. "Karl Jaspers."
    Stanford Encyclopedia of Philosophy. Stanford
    University, July 17, 2018.
    https://plato.stanford.edu/entries/jaspers/
49 "The Germans: Karl Jaspers." YouTube. YouTube,
    February 20, 2020.
    https://www.youtube.com/watch?v=tL4UuuZpAKU

50 Ibid

51 Ibid

52 Salamun, Kurt. Salamun, Jaspers' Conceptions of the
    Meaning of Life. Existenz, 2006.
    https://www.existenz.us/volumes/Vol.1Salamun.html

53 Ibid

54 Hernandez, Jill Graper. "Gabriel Marcel (1889—1973)."
    Internet Encyclopedia of Philosophy. Accessed
    March 18, 2021. https://iep.utm.edu/marcel/#H1

55 Ibid

56 Ibid

57 Zuidema, S.U. "Gabriel Marcel: A Critique," *Philosophy
    Today* 4, no. 4 (Winter 1960)

58 Hernandez, Jill Graper. "Gabriel Marcel (1889—1973)."
    Internet Encyclopedia of Philosophy. Accessed
    March 18, 2021. https://iep.utm.edu/marcel/#H2

59 Aronson, Ronald. "Albert Camus." Stanford
    Encyclopedia of Philosophy. Stanford University,
    April 10, 2017.
    https://plato.stanford.edu/entries/camus/

60 Ibid

61 Ibid

62 Ibid

63 Ibid

64 Ibid

65 Camus, Albert, and Justin O'Brien. *The Myth of Sisyphus
    and Other Essays*. New York, NY: Vintage Books,
    1955

66 Ibid

67 Ibid

68 Ibid

[69] Ibid

[70] Ibid

[71] Flynn, Thomas. "Jean-Paul Sartre." Stanford Encyclopedia of Philosophy. Stanford University, December 5, 2011. https://plato.stanford.edu/entries/sartre/

[72] Ibid

[73] Desan, Wilfrid. "Jean-Paul Sartre." Encyclopædia Britannica. Encyclopædia Britannica, inc., 2021. https://www.britannica.com/biography/Jean-Paul-Sartre

[74] Ibid

[75] Österling, Anders. "The Nobel Prize in Literature 1964 ." NobelPrize.org. Swedish Academy. Accessed March 19, 2021. https://www.nobelprize.org/prizes/literature/1964/press-release/

[76] Ibid

[77] "PHILOSOPHY - Sartre." YouTube. The School of Life, November 7, 2014. https://www.youtube.com/watch?v=3bQsZxDQgzU&ab_channel=TheSchoolofLife

[78] Ibid

[79] Ibid

[80] Ibid

[81] Ibid

[82] Ibid

[83] "Simone De Beauvoir." Encyclopædia Britannica. Encyclopædia Britannica, inc. Accessed March 19, 2021.

https://www.britannica.com/biography/Simone-de-Beauvoir

[84] Mussett, Shannon. Internet Encyclopedia of Philosophy. Accessed March 19, 2021. https://iep.utm.edu/beauvoir/#H1.

[85] "Simone De Beauvoir." Encyclopædia Britannica. Encyclopædia Britannica, inc. Accessed March 19, 2021. https://www.britannica.com/biography/Simone-de-Beauvoir

[86] Mussett, Shannon. Internet Encyclopedia of Philosophy. Accessed March 19, 2021. https://iep.utm.edu/beauvoir/#H1.

[87] Ibid

[88] "PHIL304: Existentialism, Topic: Unit 7: Simone De Beauvoir." Saylor Academy. Accessed March 19, 2021 https://learn.saylor.org/course/view.php?id=30§ionid=299

[89] Unhjem, Arne. "Paul Tillich." Encyclopædia Britannica. Encyclopædia Britannica, inc., 2020. https://www.britannica.com/biography/Paul-Tillich

[90] Ibid

[91] Ibid

[92] Manning, Russell, and Timothy Hull. "Paul Tillich by Russell Re Manning." YouTube. YouTube, June 25, 2012. https://www.youtube.com/watch?v=M_HcFLa0b1Q&ab_channel=TimelineTheologicalVideos

[93] Ibid

94 Unhjem, Arne. "Paul Tillich." Encyclopædia Britannica. Encyclopædia Britannica, inc., 2020. https://www.britannica.com/biography/Paul-Tillich

95 Manning, Russell, and Timothy Hull. "Paul Tillich by Russell Re Manning." YouTube. YouTube, June 25, 2012. https://www.youtube.com/watch?v=M_HcFLa0b1Q &ab_channel=TimelineTheologicalVideos

96 Unhjem, Arne. "Paul Tillich." Encyclopædia Britannica. Encyclopædia Britannica, inc., 2020. https://www.britannica.com/biography/Paul-Tillich

97 Ibid

98 Remanning, Russell. "Paul Tillich by Russell Remanning." YouTube. YouTube, June 25, 2012. https://www.youtube.com/watch?v=M_HcFLa0b1Q &ab_channel=TimelineTheologicalVideos

99 Ibid

100 Remanning, Russell. "Paul Tillich by Russell Remanning." YouTube. YouTube, June 25, 2012. https://www.youtube.com/watch?v=M_HcFLa0b1Q &ab_channel=TimelineTheologicalVideos

101 "Rudolf Bultmann on Demythologising Scripture Explained." New Testament Explained. YouTube, January 24, 2021. https://www.youtube.com/watch?v=bISaqrcA8Oo&a b_channel=NewTestamentExplained

102 Perrin, N. "Rudolf Bultmann." Encyclopedia Britannica, August 16, 2020. https://www.britannica.com/biography/Rudolf-Bultmann

103 Chauhan, Yamini, Gloria Lotha, Amy Tikkanen, and Priscilla Young. "University of Tübingen." Encyclopædia Britannica. Encyclopædia Britannica, inc., 2020 https://www.britannica.com/topic/University-of-Tubingen

104 Perrin, N. "Rudolf Bultmann." Encyclopedia Britannica, August 16, 2020. https://www.britannica.com/biography/Rudolf-Bultmann

105 Bultmann, Rudolf, and Hans Werner Bartsch. *Kerygma and Myth: a Theological Debate*. London, UK: SPCK, 1972

106 Arnett, W.M., "Rudolf Bultmann's Existentialist Interpretation of The New Testament", 1963. https://place.asburyseminary.edu/cgi/viewcontent.cgi?article=2051&context=asburyjournal

107 Ibid

108 Ibid

109 "Rudolf Bultmann on Demythologising Scripture Explained." New Testament Explained. YouTube, January 24, 2021. https://www.youtube.com/watch?v=bISaqrcA8Oo&ab_channel=NewTestamentExplained

110 Ibid

111 Arnett, W.M., "Rudolf Bultmann's Existentialist Interpretation of The New Testament", 1963. https://place.asburyseminary.edu/cgi/viewcontent.cgi?article=2051&context=asburyjournal

112 Ibid

113 Ibid

114 Ibid

[115] Ibid

[116] Ibid

[117] Ibid

[118] Ibid

[119] Mucai, J. (2020). *A Day in the Year 3000*. Nairobi, Kenya

BOOKS BY JOHN MUCAI

Shamba Shenanigans: A Collection of Riveting True Stories

A collection of riveting true-life experiences. Some stories are hilarious; others are thought-provoking, and others are likely to evoke different emotions as the story unfolds. Each story has one or more useful life lessons.

The Endless Search for More: A Collection of True Stories on Money Matters

A collection of true stories that revolve around our continuous search for "more." And while this trait is essential for the long-term sustainability of humanity, John Mucai suggests that we must always strive to calibrate our desires appropriately. More importantly, we should adopt a problem-solving mindset in our never-ending quest for "more."

Ngurario: A Traditional Kikuyu Marriage Experience

Ngurario is a true story of the multiple steps that John and Susan went through to formalize their marriage according to Kikuyu traditions. The book delves deeply into the drama, excitement, and joy they experienced along the way, right up to the final step in the journey, namely, an elaborate and colorful ceremony called ngurario.

Historical Snapshots of The Great: What Can We Learn from Them?

The quality of life we enjoy today is a function of the many commendable actions taken by individuals in different spheres of life. Some of these people came before us many years ago, while others live among us. This book explores the lives of some significant historical figures to determine whether they share any common attributes we can emulate.

Seeking the Right Path: A Search for Spiritual Enlightenment

This book chronicles a personal search for spiritual enlightenment. John Mucai starts by finding out what religion means.

He then looks at the different religions and zeros in on five major ones: Christianity, Islam, Hinduism, and Buddhism. These religions have a combined following, comprising about 80% of the world's population. He examines their beliefs, practices, and sacred texts.

And most importantly, the many complex questions that emerge from the texts. While the book would be of immense interest to theologians, it is not a book on theology. Instead, it is an attempt by the author to seek spiritual enlightenment by sifting through the religious literature freely available to any ordinary citizen of the world. The author's findings illuminate and hopefully give believers and non-believers a new perspective on religion.

Multiple Dilemmas: A Fictional Story of Multiple Ethical Dilemmas Based on True Historical Events

Multiple Dilemmas is a thriller based on historical events that raise significant ethical questions. The book delves deeply into challenging situations where ethical considerations are paramount, but the right choices are not clearly evident. The twists and turns in the story will keep the reader entranced for several hours.

Reminiscing on Basics: Fascinating Science and Maths Ideas for Everyone

Some ideas in science and math are so fascinating that it is a shame they are inaccessible to many people. This book attempts to fill the gap. Perhaps the curiosity triggered by these ideas will set a new intellectual journey into motion for some people, as it has done for the author.

One Day in the Year 3000

Nobody knows what the future holds one thousand years from now. But one can make some wild guesses. This book peeks into that distant future.

Stratagem: Developing A Strategic Mindset

Have you ever attended a strategy meeting and wondered whether everyone in the forum understood what strategy meant? If you have, you are not alone. Interestingly, many such meetings roll on smoothly with impressive outcomes. That phenomenon is the ninth wonder of the world. Some participants probably spend many hours after the meeting engrossed in self-doubt or guilt, depending upon how loudly they spoke during the session. A cold or hot beverage usually works wonders during such moments of self-reflection.

If you experience self-doubt but usually emerge from strategy discussions with your conscience intact, you must count your blessings. You are a brave survivor. But whatever category you belong to, you have the cure for strategy fuzziness right at your fingertips. Stratagem describes strategy with exceptional lucidity. Well-thought-out strategies are not only essential for business success; they are critical for success in personal life.

Number One: Nothing Else Seems to Count

In the modern, highly competitive world, doing well in any competition is not enough. Being number one is what counts. This book traces the lives of five colorful individuals. They are winners in their unique ways from the early stages of their lives. We intimately experience twists and turns as they enter early adulthood and get embroiled in a contest anchored in the pursuit of business success and love. At some point, each character will realize that things can become highly complex, emotionally draining, and even dangerous when love is in the mix. The outcome of their respective pursuits to be "number one" is astounding. Indeed, the way the story ends offers readers tremendous food for thought.

Fun and Grit: Encounters of Farming Hobbyists

The stories in this book are primarily about people- the people of the shamba (small farm). After working for one of the biggest multinational companies and dabbling in a small-scale farming hobby, one of my insights is that every experience, whether pleasant or unpleasant, gives life its flavor.

Indeed, some unpleasant experiences add more spice to life. Having a nice laugh about something is the magic trick in many cases. Laughter is undoubtedly the best medicine for the soul.

The Final Accounting: A Prelude to Judgment Day

The Final Accounting is a fictitious story about the preliminary interview everyone will undergo before the final judgment on Judgement Day.

Since early 2022, the world has watched with utter shock and dismay as cruelty, heartlessness, disinformation, and toxic propaganda play out on television screens and across multiple social media networks. What's astonishing is that a state of paralysis has gripped those with the power and capacity to do something about it.

However, the perpetrators will undoubtedly have to answer for their deeds during the Day of Reckoning, and even the bystanders will need to provide some answers.

This book offers the reader a humorous yet serious glimpse into how each of us will have to give a final account of our actions during our sojourn on Earth. John Mucai hopes that the book will prick the conscience of all those responsible for the craziness unfolding before our eyes almost every day, inspiring them to take action and steer things in a positive direction.

INDEX

www.ingramcontent.com/pod-product-compliance
Lightning Source LLC
Chambersburg PA
CBHW020330160726
47992CB00004B/1790